MATILDA
BONE

Also by Karen Cushman

Catherine, Called Birdy
The Midwife's Apprentice
The Ballad of Lucy Whipple
Will Sparrow's Road
Alchemy and Meggie Swann

MATILDA
BONE

Karen Cushman

HOUGHTON MIFFLIN HARCOURT
Boston   New York

Thanks to Nancy Helmbold, Professor Emeritus, Department of Classical Languages and Literatures, University of Chicago, for help with Latin, and to Robbie Cranch for her arcane knowledge, willing help, and constant friendship.

Copyright © 2000 by Karen Cushman

For information about permission to reproduce selections from this book, write to Permissions, Houghton Mifflin Harcourt Publishing Company, 215 Park Avenue South, New York, New York 10003.

www.hmhco.com

The text of this book is set in 12-point Goudy.

The Library of Congress has cataloged the hardcover edition as follows:
Cushman, Karen.
Matilda Bone/by Karen Cushman.
p. cm.
Includes bibliographical references.
Summary: Fourteen-year-old Matilda, an apprentice bonesetter and practitioner of medicine in a village in medieval England, tries to reconcile the various aspects of her life, both spiritual and practical.
[1. Physicians—Fiction. 2. Medicine—History—Fiction.
3. Middle Ages—Fiction. 4. England—Fiction.] I. Title.
PZ7.C962Mat 2000
[Fic]—dc21 00-024032
CIP   AC

ISBN: 978-0-395-88156-9 hardcover
ISBN: 978-0-547-72242-9 paperback

Manufactured in U.S.A.
DOC 10 9 8 7 6 5 4 3 2 1

4500463094

Dedicated to the memory of my fathers,
Arthur Lipski and Alvin Cushman,
and of Dorothy Briley

Contents

Arriving

 Matilda stood before the scarred wooden door and stared at the bright-yellow bone painted there. "Obviously I am here," she said softly, "and *Deus misereatur*, Lord have mercy on me."

Just a short while ago she had been mounted safe behind Father Leufredus as they had entered the stone gates of the darkening town. Then Father Leufredus said, "This is Blood and Bone Alley. I must leave you here. Nine shops along, I am told, is the place of Red Peg the Bonesetter, which will be your home now." He helped her off the horse. "*Bene vale*," he said, switching to Latin. "Farewell, Matilda. Remember all I have taught you, about right and wrong, sin and Hell, and the evils of joy and pleasure. Do always as you think I would have you do, remember your Latin, and pray ceaselessly." He blessed her and rode quickly on. She was alone.

"Please, Father," she had longed to shout at his retreating back, "please do not leave me here." She had wanted to say, "All my life you have stood between me and a world you say is dangerous and evil. How can you leave me now?" She thought to ask Saint Balbina to inflict him with boils and rashes so that he could not ride away from her, but knowing that he was a holy priest and she should obey him, she said only, "Yes, Father," as she had been taught, then added softly, "Remember to come back for me when you return from London."

Now he was gone and she stood, reluctant to go any farther. Things were going to happen, unknown things in this unknown place, and she was all unwilling and all alone. Never in her fourteen years had she been alone, there being the priest and the manor servants, the coming and going of cooks and clerks and chambermaids. And the saints, always the saints, who responded when called upon, like Saint Maurus, who had once told an unwilling Matilda, *I was able to walk on water when commanded to by my abbot. Obedience is all;* or Saint Augustine, who helped her to subdue her evil will whenever her wishes came into conflict with those of Father Leufredus. As she remembered, tears with the salty taste of winter herring slid slowly down her cheeks.

She turned and looked up and down the alley, searching for deliverance. It was a mere stub of a street off Frog Road, pocked with potholes and spattered with garbage, lined with narrow houses and shops of two stories in need of paint and repair. Many of the shops were stalls with shutters that opened upward to make an awning and down to make a counter, as was common, but some—like this one—had real, solid wooden doors, as if what went on inside was too secret and mysterious to take place in the open. There was no deliverance here.

She shivered, battered by the icy wind. Thin and small, with long yellow braids and large, wary, sea-green eyes, she stood, carrying nothing but a bundle with a change of linen—no Sunday kirtle or surcoat, no poppet or other plaything, nothing of her mother or her father or of the priest who had raised her.

Staring again at the bright-yellow bone on the door, she thought, *Bonesetter. I am to assist a bonesetter.* What would this bonesetter person be like? She imagined a saintly figure, soft-spoken and learned, who healed with but a touch of her pale, thin hands. More likely, though, the bonesetter was an ancient crone, bony and wizened, with hairy moles on her chin and cheeks, and implements of torture all about her—racks and chains and huge wooden mallets with which to crush. . . . Matilda stopped imagining and shuddered with dread. "Oh, spit and slime," she said, for they seemed the best words to express her feelings. "Spit and slime," which in Latin was *saliva mucusque*. It pleased her so well that she said it again, "*Saliva mucusque*," as she kicked at the wall of the shop with her big boot.

"Come," called a voice from within.

What had she done? The bonesetter had heard her. Matilda could picture her on the other side of the door, fingering the hairy mole on her chin.

"Come!" demanded the voice.

Matilda shifted her bundle, took a deep breath, and opened the door.

The tiny shop had a swept-dirt floor and was heated by coals glowing in a small iron brazier. There was a dark, shabby front room with table, benches, and bed with a blue coverlet, and another room beyond. The air was warm and dusty and smelled of wood smoke, sausages, goose grease, and lemon balm. Matilda entered, bumping her head against a forest of clamps and pulleys sprouting from the low ceiling. Implements of torture, just as she had imagined!

Suddenly she was grabbed from behind and swung around, her feet flying and her breath squeezed from her chest before she was plumped back onto the floor.

"I have been waiting for you, girl!" shouted a large figure looming over her.

Matilda crossed herself and backed away.

"What is wrong?" said the voice. "I am Red Peg. Are you not the Matilda come to help me?"

"I am Matilda, and you frightened me," the girl whispered. "I feared I had been snatched by the Devil."

"Do not be such a milksop. None but Peg to grab you here. Now, come and let me see you. By Theodoric the Anti-Pope, you're as welcome as the loaves and fishes." Peg moved Matilda into the weak light from the fire and peered at her. "You seem healthy enough, if a bit puny. And it's a right sweet-looking little polli-wiggle you are, with them great green eyes and a chin like God Himself had cupped it in His hand," Peg said, "but you're thin as an eel in winter."

Polliwiggle? Eel? "I am no fish," Matilda said, peering at her new mistress in the dim light: hair orange as a carrot peeping from beneath a greasy kerchief; a big smile that showed more spaces than teeth, although she appeared of no great age yet; and a face beslobbered with freckles, forehead to chin, ear to ear; tall and lean, plain, common, and most ill-mannered. Not fine and saint-ly—but no hairy moles, either. "And I am thin because I have been fasting. Father Leufredus says that God wishes us to deny our bodies for the sake of our souls."

"Great gallstones," Peg said. "God would never have created plump and meaty if He wanted us scrawny. Here, fatten up on some of these goose-liver sausages. Best that can be bought in the market, special for your coming."

As Peg eagerly sliced up the sausages, her hair popped from beneath the kerchief and frizzled about her face, but a bit of sausage grease served to hold it down once again. She licked her sticky fingers and handed a slice of sausage to Matilda.

Hungry as she was, Matilda backed away. "I cannot eat sausages."

"Whyever not?" Peg asked.

"Father Leufredus says sausages are where the butcher hides his mistakes."

Peg smiled and frowned, opened her mouth, closed it, sighed, and said, "Then leave it, and I will show you around my shop. In truth, it is not exactly mine, for it belongs to a canvas merchant who lives across town where it is cleaner and sweeter smelling. No proper merchant wants to do business on Blood and Bone Alley.

"This," she said, pounding the table with the flat of her big hand so that Matilda jumped, "is where I eat and tend to patients and where I will, God willing, beat you at draughts every night. I have a passion for draughts, my good man Tom, good friends, and sausages.

"Here is where I sleep," she continued. "You will have a pallet back there in the buttery with the pots and platters, where you'll be cozy as a yolk in an egg, and upstairs is where our landlord—thief and miser that he is—stores his overpriced canvas. There is a wee bit of a plot in the yard where we can grow a few cabbages in the summer, though mostly we will buy meat pies and onions in the street, and the baker down past the Poultry will cheat us of our pennies for bread."

A pallet on the floor? Pots and platters? Cabbages? Matilda longed to be back at the manor, where there were proper beds, beef and cheese and ale, and fires blazing in fireplaces tended by the huge, quiet Donal, or even bouncing on that bony horse headed toward London.

Peg continued to talk, describing Blood and Bone Alley, where ordinary people came to be bled, dosed, and bandaged, with its barber-surgeons down this way and leeches down that. "I am the only one on the alley setting bones," she went on, "and there has been more to do here lately than I can attend to by myself. My cousin told me there was a girl with nimble wits at Randall Manor needed a place, and I told my cousin I could use a nimble-witted girl to do as I bid her and help as necessary, and here you are. There is not overmuch to do, even for someone as little as you. . . ."

Swept by a wave of loss and loneliness, Matilda heard only the voice in her head that said over and over, *This is a miserable and lowly place with no Father Leufredus, no servants, and only sausages to eat. Oh, deliver me!*

Finally Peg ceased chattering at the girl and sent her to make ready for bed. As she spread her straw pallet on the floor, Matilda once again called for heavenly assistance: *Dear Saint Lazarus, whom Jesus raised from the dead, I do not like it here at the bonesetter's, where it is cold and dark as a tomb. I pray you rescue me.*

My child, she heard the saint replying, *I understand your unhappiness, for I too was left in a cold, dark tomb. Of course, I was dead. Have courage.*

Looking for Deliverance

 Matilda heard rain slapping against the roof as she woke. With no window unshuttered, she could not tell if it was dusk or dawn outside, just that it was near dark inside. Not knowing where she was at first, she was bewildered, but found she preferred that to the hopeless, lonely feeling that came next. "Blood and Bone Alley," she said to herself. "I am somewhere named Blood and Bone Alley, with a mistress who is noisy, untidy, and not at all holy. And I am miserably cold." She tucked her icy hands beneath her as she watched her breath steam in the frigid air for a moment.

The room grew very gradually lighter, although no warmer. Morning, then. Matilda said her morning prayers, leapt up, pulled on her shift and kirtle, and jumped back into bed. "I think the fire must have gone out," she said to herself, "for even in this place it would never otherwise be so cold."

Getting up again, she hopped and jumped over the icy floor to the brazier in the front room. Peg was but a hump under the blue coverlet.

"There is no fire, Mistress Peg," Matilda called.

"Just as I expected," said Peg, her voice muffled by the coverlet, "for you are to tend the fire."

"The fire? Me?"

Peg sat up, her wild red hair standing out like flames around a martyred saint. "You. Were you not listening to me last night? I clearly said that you would be obliged to tend the fire."

"Is there no slavey or servant to do that?"

"Yes, indeed. You. Now stop squeaking at me or we will surely freeze to death. You will find kindling wood in a box in the buttery and some nice bits of charcoal. I think there is enough fire left in those embers to raise a blaze without much trouble," said Peg, pulling the blue coverlet over her head again.

Matilda gathered up the wood and charcoal and carried it into the front room, where she dumped it in a heap on the gray coals in the brazier. Ash flew up into her eyes, her hair, her mouth.

"I am smothered near to death," she said. "And my kirtle is stained with sap and ash. I cannot do this."

"I was told you are uncommonly clever," came Peg's voice. "Surely you can make a simple fire."

Matilda took a wooden spoon in her frozen fingers and began to stir the mess in the brazier, gently blowing as she had seen Donal do at the manor. Ashes flew into the air like dusky snowflakes but, *Deo gratias*, the fire lighted. Also the wooden spoon. She opened the door and threw it out into the rain, where it spluttered and lay black and jagged in the mud. Closing the door, she called, "The fire is lit."

She sat down on the bench, crossed her hands on the table, and waited. She had forgone supper last night and was mightily hungry. Her guts grumbled. Finally she asked Peg, "When will there be breakfast?"

A loud sigh came from under the blue coverlet. "When you prepare something."

No doubt, Matilda thought, *I will also be expected to empty the chamber pots and pick the weevils from the bread*. She sat still, clenching her jaw to hold her misery in, missing Father Leufredus, warm ale and cheese for breakfast, all that was familiar to her.

Peg got up, dressed, and dropped a loaf of yesterday's hard bread on the table in front of Matilda. "Eat. You can start tomorrow." She sat down across from the girl and broke off a bit of bread. "I know something of your story from my cousin, who is brother-in-law to

Lord Randall's clerk—how you lost your parents long ago and were raised at the manor," she said, chewing. "Tell me what you did there and what you know."

"What I did *not* have to do," said Matilda, taking a big breath and a small piece of bread, "was light fires. Or eat sausages."

"Never? What then did you do?"

The girl took a bite of the hard bread and chewed industriously. "I had reading and writing, Latin and Greek, from my father. And Father Leufredus taught me to seek higher things, like God and Heaven, saintliness and obedience. We prayed, and he taught me about God and the Devil, Heaven and Hell. I read aloud from the lives of the saints when he was tired, did some writing and figuring for him, kept his papers in order and his holy books. I was of much assistance to him."

"Yet this Father Leufredus left you."

"God and the Church called him to London to swear his support to the young king who is Edward the Third. And Lord Randall's clerk's brother-in-law contrived to send me to you. I do not know why I could not accompany Father Leufredus or await his return at the manor. But I could not." Matilda stopped, suddenly overwhelmed by loneliness.

Peg jumped into the silence. "Well, and now you

are here, where you will be of much assistance to *me*," she said. "Let me see your hands."

Matilda held out her small hands, their broad palms and straight fingers stained with ink. "Bonesetting is a skill of the hands," Peg said, examining them front and back. "You seem fine as fivepence to me—smart and strong enough to be a right skillful workfellow to a bonesetter, for all you're little as a flea. In exchange for your doing what I need done, I will give you an occasional penny and your keep."

"As I have said," Matilda responded, still frowning at being likened to a flea, "I assisted Father Leufredus with reading and writing and figuring. Perhaps I could do the same here."

"I have little enough use for figuring and none for writing. As to reading, why only last year Geoffrey Blackhead, the bishop's clerk, was reading from the letters of John of Salisbury as he walked along the riverbank and right into the water. Nothing was ever seen of him again but for his hat, which floated downriver as far as Toadapple Village." Peg crossed herself. "No, there will be no reading here. What I need is someone to tend the fire, see to meals, brew lotions and boil tonics, soothe and restrain patients, and help me in the setting of bones."

Brew and boil? Restrain? Matilda felt hopelessness

descend like a weight on her shoulders. She was here in the wrong place with the wrong mistress until Father Leufredus came to rescue her.

"There'll be no one in town can teach you as much about bonesetting as old Red Peg here," Peg went on. "I have been setting bones on the alley since I was apprentice to Harold Spinecracker, many years ago." Peg crossed herself again. "Harold is now setting bones in Heaven, the Lord bless him for a sweet and noble soul."

She swept most of the bread crumbs onto the floor. "What we call bonesetting," she said, "is the freeing of stiff or injured limbs, the mending of broken or ill-formed ones. Folk come with pains or aches, fever sometimes, red and swollen joints sometimes, or leg or arm frozen from disuse. We'll see children overridden by ale carts and left with broken limbs, clumsy carpenters who tripped or fell or hammered their fingers instead of nails, men and women crippled by disease. If it has to do with bones or joints, Red Peg is the person to see. Twenty years or more it has now been, and I have tended to every finger, back, and knee in this town."

Matilda frowned. Surely God had sent such suffering and should be the one to see to its release, not this woman. And certainly not Matilda, who yearned for higher things.

"What we do," Peg continued, "depends on what we think wrong. Bonesetting is also a skill of the brain." She smiled at Matilda. "Come here and I will show you." Peg reached for the girl.

Matilda backed away and crossed herself.

"By the broken bones of Saint Stephen!" Peg shouted. "Just what has you trembling and quaking now? Are you still afeared of the Devil grabbing you?"

"No, I am afeared of *you* grabbing me. Will this hurt?"

"Not a jot. Just hasten on up here," said Peg with a soft whack on the girl's rump, "and lie on your back."

Matilda very slowly climbed up onto the table, brushing away the remaining bread crumbs, sausage leavings, and other dusty, lumpy substances. Peg pulled clamps from the ceiling, measured Matilda's height with a critical eye, and chose a section of rope. She attached the clamps to the girl's leg with ropes and pulleys.

Matilda recoiled, inhaling with a hiss. Peg's hands felt warm and strong, but she was not used to being touched.

"If there is aught you do not understand, just ask me. Anytime," said Peg. "Now we begin.

"Fractures are breaks in the bones. We pull the edges apart, straighten the bones, and push the pieces back into place. Then we must hold them together until they mend." Using the girl's skinny leg for a model, Peg showed her how to pack the limb with comfrey root and wrap it in wet leather that would shrink as it dried to act as a splint. "Here," Peg said, "watch how I thread the ropes through this pulley to break down a stiffened joint." And she demonstrated how to restrain struggling patients and how to sit atop those having ill-mended breaks rebroken to keep them from shifting or running away. Peg bounced once, and the girl said, "Oof" and then "Oof!" She was smarting and sore when Peg released her from the table.

"You will also be brewing our lotions, potions, tonics, and ointments. The dried herbs are kept in these crocks by the table. See, here is comfrey, also called boneset. Here, houseleeks and nightshade berries, watercress and wormwood. And sicklewort for stanching cuts. You'll soon learn which is which. Always be careful to use only what I tell you. Do as I do." She added herbs to a kettle and hung it over the fire. "This is horseradish to boil with grease for a liniment. Stir it carefully and watch it closely. And never let the mixture boil over."

She treats me like a kitchen maid, thought Matilda. *As if I am fit for nothing but measuring and brewing. Why, I know Latin and French and some Greek, as well as*

reading and writing and figuring. I can name the three
wise men, the seven deadly sins, and a great many of
the 133,306,668 devils of Hell: Abaddon, Abduscius,
Abigor . . .

The mixture boiled over onto the dirt floor.

"You beef-brained ninny!" shouted Peg. "You could
have roasted yourself! And now it has gone to waste.
Here. Pour what is left into this jug."

Matilda tipped the kettle and spilled the remaining
liquid.

"It seems I have made a bad bargain," Peg said,
grabbing the kettle. "You are not good for much."

Matilda's stomach knotted with fear. She would
not want Father Leufredus to come back and find her
in disfavor. Or what if this hard woman turned her out?
She had nowhere to go until he returned. With tears in
her eyes she said softly, "Please, Mistress Peg, show me
again. I will attend carefully."

Peg, her face red with anger and teeth clenched,
said, "Perhaps we should start with something easier.
Now, watch closely." She stuck her own sturdy leg up
on the bench and rolled the stocking down to her
ankle. "For those who are overworked or suffer the
pains of old age or need a gentle touch, I rub a bit of
monkshood oil into the joints, like this, and wrap
them to keep them warm. Beware, however, my girl.

Like meekness, holiness, and clumsiness, monkshood oil can be overdone."

Matilda looked up quickly. Was Peg mocking her? Or jesting? Or was she telling her something important?

Peg stood up and continued. "We do not brew the monkshood oil here. My Tom brings it when he comes." Her face softened. "Tom, now, he travels, comes and goes like the rheumatics. Ten years we have been wed, and still I miss him when he is gone. He betakes himself here and there sharing his knowledge and instructing others. My Tom is a man of learning, wise, clever, and well-mannered."

"A man of learning?" Matilda repeated, suddenly attentive.

"Oh, yes. A great man."

"It is well that he is a great man," Matilda said, "but Father Leufredus advises against earthly attachments, for they take our minds away from God and Heaven."

"Well, everyone prefers a different sort of cheese, I suppose," said Peg.

What a thing to say! Matilda looked at the woman in surprise and horror. If Father Leufredus could hear her! The priest would be appalled at this blasphemy. But he would not wish Matilda to argue with her mistress, so Matilda said only, "Where might I be alone to pray?"

"Right now?"

"Father Leufredus instructed me to pray seven times each day, standing, kneeling, or prostrate on the floor, with arms—"

"I go to Bertrand Buttercrambe's to tend his leg, for he cannot be moved," said Peg. "Scrub down the table and you may have this room until dinner. You have learned enough this morning." And she left the shop muttering, "Would I could adjust a person's thinking with ropes and pulleys as easily as I can a fractured leg."

Matilda, lying on the floor with arms outstretched, frowned at the hearing, thinking Peg hurtful, heretical, and much too heavy for sitting on folk.

CHAPTER THREE

Going to Market

 "After that unsatisfactory breakfast I am more than ready for dinner," said Peg when she returned.

"And I," added Matilda.

Peg said nothing but pulled a small brass knife from beneath her belt and began to clean the dirt and goose grease from under her fingernails. Finally Matilda sighed and, fearing the answer, asked Peg softly, "What are we eating and when are we eating it?"

"We are eating what you buy in the market, and we are eating it when you bring it home and cook it."

"I cannot."

"Maybe in Heaven," said Peg, "food buys and cooks itself, but on earth someone must do it. And here in my shop that someone is you."

"But I do not know how to buy food or cook it."

"Why not?"

"At the manor others did that. I am no kitchen maid. I seek higher things."

"You had better seek fish heads or chicken pies, else there will be no dinner. Get what is fresh and cheap. And bread. And maybe a cabbage or a ginger cake."

Peg gave Matilda three pennies and directions to the market. Matilda said, "Yes, Mistress Peg," but did not listen as she pulled on her boots and cloak. She had no idea where the market was, but if someone as lowly and uneducated as Mistress Peg could find it, so too could Matilda.

A gusty wind rattled shutters and set shop signs swinging as Matilda walked up the alley and turned onto Frog Road. She looked carefully about her, for she had arrived in near darkness and had not seen this town, this Chipping Bagthorpe, halfway between London and Oxford but near to neither. It was the first time she had been over a mile from the place where she was born. *I never knew*, she thought, *there were so many people in the world, so many roads*. And so many buildings: houses and shops crowded together, leaning higgledy-piggledy against each other and away, to the left and to the right; taverns and inns, dark and crowded and ominous; churches with their bell towers pointing up to Heaven.

What if I lost my way in this place? she thought, dazed by it all. *I could starve to death around the corner from a baker, die unshriven down the road from a church, and never know.*

Taking a deep breath, she turned right past the Church of Saint Zoe the Martyr, who had been hanged from a tree by her hair before being roasted like a snipe, Matilda knew. The streets grew more crowded. Peddlers called out, advertising their meager winter wares: onions and turnips, apples only slightly withered, salt meat, salt fish, salt! Church bells clamored from every street corner. Beggars whined, dogs barked, pigs snorted as they rooted in the refuse. "Have you any rats to kill?" cried one tradesman. "Or clothes to mend?" called another as Matilda walked by.

She went left two streets, up past the well, and around the corner, trying to avoid the occasional housewife emptying her chamber pot out the window, then past the Church of Saint Zoe the Martyr, and then . . .

Matilda stopped and looked around. Saint Zoe? Again? What now? Straight ahead? Left or right? Matilda prayed for a sign, like the moon on fire or a two-headed horse. But, it being day, there was no moon, and all the horses she saw had but one head.

She turned and went past the Church of Saint Zoe

the Martyr once more, three streets the other way, through the Street of the Cupmakers and past the Church of Saint Zoe the Martyr. *"Saliva mucusque!"* said Matilda as she turned again and went four blocks left, past Shoemakers' Street, up along the river to Fish Street, and finally there was the market square.

The rain had stopped for a time, and the square was packed with people, bundled up in woolen scarves and gloves, buying and selling, begging and thieving. Never before had Matilda been to a market. Her nose filled with the smell of beeswax candles, fine perfumes, onions, and nutmeg. She pulled her cloak tighter against the wind as she paused to watch the magicians, acrobats, and jugglers. She lingered at the silk stall and the leather booths, lost in the sights and sounds and smells, until her stomach rumbled a loud, hungry rumble. *A chicken,* she thought. It was not Lent, and she was not fasting today. Father Leufredus would approve of a chicken. *Let us have a chicken, then, fat and juicy and golden from the fire.*

She turned toward the Poultry, where chickens lashed together by their feet hung squawking and wriggling from the beams of the stalls. "How much for a chicken?" she asked the poultryman.

"Three pennies."

It was all she had. There would be no bread or

cabbage. She thought again of the chicken, roasted golden.

"One chicken," she said. "Kindly kill it and pluck it clean."

The poultryman laughed. "You bought it, you kill and pluck it," he said, handing her a chicken by its feet. She reached out warily to grab it. The chicken squawked, Matilda squealed, and she dropped it as though it were on fire. The chicken made its escape amid baskets of duck feet and wild partridges.

"Where are my pennies?" asked the poultryman.

"Where is my chicken?" asked Matilda softly as she walked quickly away. The poultryman cursed loud and vulgar curses as he jumped over the duck feet in his haste to get his chicken back.

"Obviously God did not intend for us to have a chicken for dinner. Perhaps something easier and already dead," said Matilda to herself. She headed back to Fish Street to find a fishmonger's stall.

There were so many kinds of fish. "I need for dinner some fish that is fresh and cheap," she said to the pock-faced man at the stall.

"Do you know much about fish?" asked the fishmonger, looking hard at her.

"Oh, yes," said Matilda. "Fish escaped God's curse on the earth by dwelling in the water and thus are blessed among living things. The fish is the symbol of Saint Peter, who was a fisherman, and Saint Zeno of Verona. We are allowed to eat fish during Lent and on other fast days when meat is forbidden."

"But do you know what fish is good to eat?"

"No," Matilda admitted.

"Then it is your happy fortune that you came to me, for some others would try to cheat you. You can trust me." The fish man smiled a smile empty of teeth but full of guile. "The best fish for eating is the eel, and," he said, lowering his voice, "I have a special one here. See how big his head is—means he was sharp-witted and wise. Eating a wise fish makes *you* wise. And his skin is that mottled brown that means he is ripe. I will give you this eel for . . . how much do you have?"

"Three pennies."

He shook his head. "This eel is worth much more than three pennies. I cannot sell it for so little. Oh, well," he said, with a great sigh, "you look so little and so hungry. Here, take it for three pennies. Take it and go. Quickly. Quickly. And show no one, for they will all rush to my stall looking for a bargain to equal yours." He took her pennies, wrapped the eel in wet grass, and handed it to Matilda.

She stepped back. "It smells so strongly of fish," she said.

"Strong smell means fresh fish," said the fishmonger. "Do you not know the saying?"

Matilda shook her head, took her eel, and left.

On her way back to Peg's, near as tortuous a route as that she had taken to the market, people crossed the road to avoid walking near her, but she did not notice as she was occupied pretending to be Saint Doucelina floating three feet off the ground in ecstasy.

As she turned onto Frog Road, she saw a crowd following behind an impressive-looking man in black surcoat lined with fur and embroidered red shoes. At his waist was a leather belt, from which dangled a small book bound in gold and russet. He looked learned. And worthy. And clean.

"Who," she asked one of the crowd, "is that man?"

"It is Theobald, the physician," she was answered.

"Master Theobald the Wonderworker," said someone else. And yet another person said, "It is that Theobald who saved the Lord Mayor's life by dosing him with pepper and spikenard and sitting on his stomach."

Matilda watched him with awe.

He was approached by a well-padded woman—a goose girl, perhaps, or a butcher's wife—with a broad red face, strong teeth, and feet like mandolins. "Master Theobald," the woman said, "I am come again to beseech you. You say I am not worthy to physick. Then teach me. Or assist me. Or—"

"I do not teach those who can read neither Latin nor the stars," the master physician said, wrapping his cloak about him. "Nor those who are loud or blasphemous. Nor women." The crowd murmured in agreement.

"I have just seen a woman give birth to a dead son and three days later follow him to Heaven or Hell," the red-faced woman responded. "I dosed and cleansed, patched and prodded, watched and listened, held her and sang as sweetly as I could. I used massage, rare stones, tansy wine, holy amulets, prayer, everything I know. For nothing. Her life poured out of her with the blood that drenched her pallet. How would your reading and your Aristotle have changed that?"

"I believe the answer must lie in the stars. Perhaps she chose to begin her labor at an ill-omened moment—"

"*Chose!* As if a woman could choose when to begin labor!"

The man turned to leave. "Wait, Master Theobald. Wait," the woman called. His steps slowed. "I am sorry for my temper. Let us say perhaps she did choose to begin labor at a less than propitious time. What then could I have done to save her? Help me! Teach me!"

"Read Galen and Aristotle," he said as he walked away.

"Galen and Aristotle," she muttered. "If he wants to know whether a frog has teeth, does he read Aristotle and Galen on frogs? I want to know what *he* knows, not what dead men have said."

Matilda watched the physician disappear, the goose girl calling, "Master Theobald! Master!" as she ran after him. Father Leufredus always said, "Learned authority is more true than mere experience." No doubt that was what made this Master Theobald a great man. Anyone could look in the frog's mouth.

Matilda sighed. *Would that I had been sent as attendant to this great and learned doctor instead of the loud and unholy Peg*, she thought as she walked on.

Encountering Doctor Margery

 "What do we have for dinner?" asked Peg when Matilda returned.

"Eel," said Matilda, flopping it onto the table.

"And what else? Cabbage? Onions? Parsley? Bread?"

"Just eel, Mistress Peg. It took all the pennies, but I made a good bargain." She unwrapped the fish.

The door opened and closed. "What is that loathsome smell?" asked a voice Matilda had heard before. It was the goose girl from the street.

"Dinner, dear Margery," said Peg, "purchased by my new and useless helper, who hasn't the wit to know rotten fish." Peg shoved Matilda forward.

Matilda's face burned. She longed to hide, be gone, vanish altogether.

"Were you not put off by the reek?" Peg asked her.

"Strong smell means fresh fish, he said," Matilda told Peg.

"He said this was fresh?"

"Yes, Mistress Peg."

"A fresh eel has a white belly, a small head, glistening skin, and a mild salty smell. This eel was neither sound when alive nor edible now." She shook her head. "How much did he ask for it?"

"Three pennies."

"And how much did you pay?"

"Three pennies!"

"For that reeking eel? You were cheated mightily." Peg sighed. "Never give what is asked at first. And never buy an eel with a big head. Throw this into the alley for the cats. We will have porridge for dinner."

Matilda opened the door. She wished to disappear into the alley with the stinking fish. To be made to do lowly things, and then to fail! She sighed loudly as she tossed the fish out, slammed the door, and turned back toward Peg and the goose girl.

Peg poured grains and water into a kettle and hung it over the fire for a porridge. "This," said Peg to Matilda as she stirred, "is our physician, Margery Lewes—a woman, of course, for no true physician would work here on the alley with barbers and bonesetters."

"True physicians work where the streets are cleaner, the houses larger, and the fees bigger," said Margery, laughing a laugh like the screech of a rusty cart wheel as she sat down on the bench.

"But woman though she be," Peg continued, "she is physician indeed. Have you fever or boils? Fallen arches or wambly gut? Marg here can mend them all."

A physician! Matilda measured the woman with her eyes the way Peg had measured the rope for the pulley. The short, stout Margery could not possibly be a physician! No wonder her patient had died.

"Tell me, sweet Margery," Peg said, placing bowls and spoons on the table, "what comes of your wooing of the great Theobald?"

"Little enough. I saw him just a few moments ago and chased him through half the streets of this town, begging and cajoling, to no use. Theobald will not help me, nor send me patients, nor agree to offer whatever instruction he thinks I need. God's wounds!" Margery said, banging her fist on the table so that the spoons danced. "It is bad enough I must go crawling to Theobald because he is the city's leading physician, but worse to be turned away. I will speak no more of this. Tell me some news."

"Old Agnes sold a love potion to the sheriff and was taken as a witch," Peg said.

Margery frowned. "Perhaps more cheerful news."

"I saw Nathaniel Cross at the butcher's in the east market yestermorn. He and Sarah have taken in yet another stray cat and her kittens."

Matilda stood listening. What kind of place was this? she wondered. Blood and Bone Alley. Goose girls who masquerade as physicians. People who consort with cats. Matilda could hear the cats outside the door fighting over the eel she had thrown there. She hated cats. Father Leufredus said a cat was more likely a witch than an animal and refused to bless a house with a cat in it. *Saliva mucusque!* she thought. *Do these people know nothing of the Devil and his creatures? For certain the air will be corrupted and we will fall dead in fevers and consumptions.* Matilda crossed herself. And then again.

"Don't you be mocking Nathaniel, Marg my dear," Peg was saying. "I warrant his gooseberry liniment and sweet temper have done more to soothe the aches and pains of this town than all my pushing and pulling."

"You ever did have a sweet spot for Nathaniel, Peg."

"In truth I do, for his is the best soul God ever made." Peg turned to Matilda. "Nathaniel has suffered much these last years. His good wife is sore sickly, and his own eyes are failing him, yet still he is sweet and comforting as honey wine. But as Margery knows well, my Tom is the only man for me." Peg patted Margery on her arm. "Mayhap you, dear Marg, should start looking for a man of your own. Might dull that sharp tongue of yours."

Saint Paul did say it was better to marry than to burn, thought Matilda, *although who would ever marry that goose girl I do not know.* She snorted as she pictured this Margery bedecked in bridal finery.

Peg and Margery looked at Matilda, who felt her cheeks flame. Margery cleared her throat and said, "Good day to you, Peg. And good fortune. She seems a bit unusual, your pious new servant girl."

"The cook fire is calling the candle hot, dear Margery," said Peg with a laugh.

Margery winked, turned, and left, kicking up little dust storms as she hurried to the door. Matilda frowned at her departing back. Servant girl? She was here to attend to Peg, not to be a scullion.

Peg looked at Matilda's frown and said tartly, "Mistress Margery, whatever you may think, is twice the physician, three times the person, and at least four times a better soul than that person who calls himself Master Theobald or any other hundred people I could name."

"Of course, Mistress Peg," Matilda said. *I sincerely doubt it, Mistress Peg*, Matilda thought.

CHAPTER FIVE

Tending a Cat

 Alkelda Weaver from Acorn-under-Bridgewater brought in her baby daughter, whose right leg had been broken in a fall from her cradle some months before. The leg had been set by the village barber but was healing crookedly, so the right foot pointed west while the left pointed north. It was so cold in the shop that ice shone in the cracks on the wall, and the cracks in Peg's work-worn hands bled; still, she examined the baby's tiny bones slowly and gently.

"Why do you trouble yourself about such matters?" Matilda asked hesitantly as Peg moved the right foot back and forward. "Could you not call on the saints for help? Saints Victor and Peter and Servais are said to be excellent for foot trouble. Surely they would cure her, were it God's will."

"God gave me this brain and these hands to *do* His

will, I think," said Peg, "and by Saint Elmo's elbow, I plan to do my best."

Matilda frowned in confusion. She could find nothing to dispute in Peg's statement, yet she felt sure that Father Leufredus would not agree with it.

"Watch what I do," Peg said to Matilda. She rubbed the child's leg with colewort ointment, goose grease, and ginger, then pulled and pushed. "We must loosen the joint that has healed crooked and get her foot used to turning another way." Peg sang over and over, "Tumbling toadflax and pimpernel, soon your leg will be all well," but the little girl cried with pain.

Matilda was appalled. *Dear Saint Hippolytus, who knew suffering,* she prayed, *please deliver this child from her torture at the hands of the bonesetter.* But the saint replied, *You consider this torture? Why, I was tied by my feet to a team of horses and dragged through thistles and thorns. That was torture! This is healing. Watch and learn.*

So Matilda watched, and finally it was over. Peg told Alkelda Weaver, "Bring her to see me every week, and mayhap we can have the right foot facing northwest at the least." Then she set out the remains of the bread and sausage for mother and daughter.

"I gave our dinner to Alkelda Weaver," said Peg to Matilda later, "for they have a long, hungry walk back to their village. Put water to boil for porridge."

As she listened to her empty stomach grumble, Matilda wished that Mistress Peg would think of others who might be hungry before she gave their dinner away. Or that she would run out of porridge. Or that she could miraculously produce food, as did the blessed Saint Brigid. Thinking about Saint Brigid reminded her of rainy afternoons at the manor hearing Father Leufredus tell about the lives of the saints: Saint Hormisdas, who cleaned the camel stables; Simeon Stylites, who lived atop a pillar; the holy martyrs Agatha and Agnes and Athanasius the Fuller. Matilda sat down on the bench. Time went on.

Peg came in from the buttery. "What has my useless helper been about all this time, sitting in here?"

Matilda jumped up. "I am thinking about saints."

"You mean you are doing nothing? Letting moss grow on you? Where is the water for porridge? Why is the floor not swept?"

Matilda grabbed the broom. Sweeping? How unimportant, lowly, and unholy! How could Peg dare criticize her piety? Could Peg not see her concern for Heaven, for doing what was commanded, for pleasing God and Father Leufredus? She felt she had fallen among barbarians, who neither understood nor wished to understand but disagreed with her even so. Father Leufredus *must* come back for her! To that end Matilda called on Saint Ambrose of Milan for help, but the saint answered, *I am fully occupied being the patron of bishops and beekeepers and do not have the time to come to your assistance. I suggest you discover who aids those who attend to bonesetters and do not bother me.*

"*Saliva mucusque,*" said Matilda as she rubbed her hands, red and sore from the rough handle of the broom.

Later, when the porridge was still a lump in her gut, there came an impatient knocking at the door. "Will no one let us in? Must I stand here all day?" a voice called.

"Old Mother Uffa," said Peg, "who has the little house at the end of the alley. Open the door for her."

The woman at the door was old enough to be Methuselah's mother, with a face as russet and wrinkled as last year's apple. Her small body was twisted and bent, and there on her chin was the wart Matilda had once imagined on Peg.

As Peg helped her to the table, Mother Uffa croaked, "Keep your quackish hands off me. Naught wrong with Mother Uffa, but Hag here has a bad leg." The old woman opened her cloak to reveal the patient.

Matilda was horror-struck. Hag was a cat—an old, ugly, skinny cat, with patches of pink skin showing through her brownish fur and a tail that bent in the middle as though God had changed His mind in the fashioning of it. She yawned in Matilda's face, exhibiting both her one remaining tooth and breath that reminded Matilda of her bargain eel.

"Well, old dear," said Peg, taking up the cat, "let's see what ails you." While Mother Uffa complained about the butcher, the Lord Mayor, the King, and even Peg herself, Peg gently examined the cat's leg.

"Hag is an exceptional cat," said Peg to Matilda as Hag bit her probing fingers. "Most evil-tempered animal in the alley. And very important to Mother Uffa. We must do what we can."

It was bad enough, Matilda thought, to be occupied with the unsaintly business of pushing and pulling bones. But a *cat!* A creature with no soul that consorted with devils and ate rats! She would not touch it, she vowed. How would she ever explain this to Father Leufredus?

"Ah, here," Peg said. "The leg is broken. I can feel the two edges. A clean break. Matilda, prepare the comfrey as I showed you. We will pack it across the break and bind it with linen cloth to help the bone heal together again."

"But a *cat* . . ."

"Matilda! The comfrey!"

Matilda drained the comfrey pulp and handed it to

Peg with a frown. Peg packed it around the break and wrapped the leg in linen strips to hold it immobile.

"There, old girl," said Peg to Hag. "Take heart. You'll be running and jumping again before you can say 'Saint Cadwaladr.'"

"How much?" asked Mother Uffa.

"You owe me nothing," said Peg.

"I pays my way."

"Well, then, I will take a kitten from Hag's next litter."

Mother Uffa agreed, picked up Hag, and left the shop cackling.

"I think you were cheated," said Matilda to Peg. "How can you be sure that cat will have kittens?"

"She won't. She is much too old," said Peg. "Did you think I really wanted one?"

Matilda was confused by Peg's logic but even more concerned for Peg's soul. "Truly you should not be treating cats, Mistress Peg. Father Leufredus says a cat is *cane pejor et angue*. That means worse than a dog or a snake."

"By Saint Kentigern's salmon, you are so priest-ridden that one might think you have nothing of your own to say."

Of course I do, Matilda thought, *but I try not to say it*. Father Leufredus wished her to subdue her will to God's. And to his. And she struggled to do so.

Never had she felt so alone. If only she could talk with her holy priest, she would be comforted, but she could not. If she had skins and ink, she could write to him, but she had not.

The next day when she was sent to the market ("Cheese," said Peg. "No mold. Not over a penny's worth. And an onion. Fresh."), Matilda took her bundle of belongings with her. After securing the cheese and onion, she sought out a parchment seller. Many questions led her to the shop of a crippled widow, Juliana Parchmenter, who agreed to trade writing supplies for what Matilda had. Finally they settled on a linen shift and a pair of stockings: it was all Matilda owned except for what she wore. Though the parchment page was rough and marred with small holes, there was also a pot of good black ink and a goose-quill pen. Matilda ran back to Peg's with her purchases.

After their cheese-and-onion supper, Matilda broke the ice in the jug, washed her hands and face, and knelt shivering on the floor, her unbraided hair falling about her like a river of ripening barley. *Pater noster*, she said, and *O Deus meus*, and *Benedictus qui*, all the customary prayers learned so carefully at the side of Father Leufredus. Then finally she was able to sit on her pallet and write a letter, in her best Latin and finest calligraphy. *At St. Werburga's Church, London, the right godly and worshipful Father Leufredus,* she wrote,

I recommend me to you, beseeching your blessing and your heedfulness. I helped to doctor a cat today. I pray God will forgive me. I did not choose to do it but was compelled by Peg. She is teaching me bonesetting, at which, I must admit, she does have some skill and experience. And she does not seem especially wicked, except for her hair, which is the Devil's own red, although she is unholy and most wrong at times. But a cat! I am exceedingly confused by this world. What I know to be true and valuable and right is counted as little here, and what I know to be wrong-headed is approved.

I continue to do as you have taught me, to pray and meekly obey, but still I fear my soul is in danger. I can almost smell the foul breath of the mighty goat-horned Satan, who sits by my bed, waiting to snatch me with his sharp claws, the moment I forget my Latin or take my eyes from Heaven, and sweep me off to Hell, where fire falls from the sky like rain. May it please you, could you please come back for me soon?

By your humble pupil,
Matilda

She put the letter under her pallet and lay down to sleep. On nights like this, when the fear of Hell chilled her soul, Matilda liked to imagine her arrival in Heaven. The great and holy ones would be there to greet her: Saints Peter and Paul, Patrick, Praetextatus, Vincent, Scholastica and Cunegund, and Saint Lucy carrying her eyes on a platter. Matilda used to imagine arriving on a creamy white horse, but after the hard and bony seat she had suffered all the way from Lower Woadmarsh, she now preferred to picture herself in a litter with scarlet silk curtains all around. God, seated on a big chair with an embroidered footstool, would call impatiently, "Bring her here. To me. Hurry. Hurry. I have waited so long." And He would seat her right next to Him—God, with His white hair, and fine, noble hands, and Father Leufredus's face.

The next morning she went to the Church of Saint Zoe the Martyr. Seeking out the priest, she explained her situation. "I must get word to Father Leufredus. Could you keep this letter for me and send it next time you meet someone going to London?"

The priest agreed, blessed her, and blew his nose in the sleeve of his cassock, so touched was he by her story.

Leeching

 "There," said Peg, wiping her hands on her skirt. "Now take those soft hands of yours to Grizzl's and rub her just as I showed you."

Matilda went first to the shop of Horanswith Leech, the bloodletter, at the end of Blood and Bone Alley where it met Frog Road. As many times as she had passed his shop and crossed herself in apprehension, she had never been inside nor seen the dreaded bloodletter. She walked slowly, kicking at stones and bones and things, anxious to delay her arrival as long as possible.

The door to Horanswith Leech's home was barred, and no one answered her knocking. Relieved for the moment, Matilda sat on an upturned herring barrel and waited. Too soon came a man in dusty black gown and mantle, spotted with mud and blood and a year's worth of spilled dinners. He looked much like a leech himself, his thin little hands like pincers and teeth sharp enough to draw blood. On his head he wore what looked like a yellow clay pot.

"Is it me you want?" he asked.

"If you are the leech," Matilda said, staring at the . . . hat? pot? helmet? crown?

He took the object off his head, freeing his black hair, dusty and coarse as a horse's. "Bleeding bowl, you see," he said. "Easier to carry. Keeps my hands free." Horanswith Leech, without doubt.

Matilda followed him into the gloomy room that was his home and shop. It smelled of blood and dirt and insects.

"Busy, busy. What's the reason? It be early blood-letting season," he said. "Everyone wants to be bled before spring. You also, pretty thing?"

Matilda shuddered, both at the thought of bleeding and at his dreadful rhymes. She shook her head. "Mistress Peg asks that you and I go to Grizzl Wimplewasher by the river. She suffers from aches in her hands and feet and those places where two bones rub together. You are to bleed Grizzl and I to apply this liniment."

Horanswith Leech grinned, his tiny sharp teeth glowing in the gloom. "Excellent, excellent, for whatever ailment." He looked at the girl closely. "I perceive that you truthfully wonder how bleeding could possibly help her."

Matilda nodded.

"You know four humors rule the body in any circumstance: blood, phlegm, and black and yellow bile, which must be kept in balance," said Horanswith Leech to Matilda. "Illness or pain, if I may be redundant, means one of the humors is superabundant. Or even double. Too much blood is the cause of most trouble."

"And bleeding?" asked Matilda.

"Reduces pains, without a doubt, once we let the extra blood out. For one of Grizzl's age and condition, I think the leeches. We won't open a vein, which a bit overreaches."

Matilda shivered as Master Leech took the cover off a large pottery crock. "My beauties, we have work to do. Come, Arelda, Maude, and Gerty, too. Time to work, Agrippina, Felix, Basil, Thomelinus. We'll have her up and dancing between us." He picked up the wriggling black leeches one by one and dropped them into a leather pouch, put his bowl on his head, and hurried out the door. Fearful and disgusted but curious, Matilda followed.

Matilda trailed Horanswith Leech so closely that

she saw little but his black woolen back flapping down Frog Road, around the market, to the river, and past three bridges until they came to a cottage small as an overturned wagon, made of mud and straw. Grizzl stood before her door, stirring a great mass of wet linen in a large iron pot. "Ah, good, you are here," she said. "Peg told me you would surely come." She straightened, rubbed her red hands together, coughed a time or two, and said, "Go in out of this chill. I will be there as soon as I hang these to dry—as well as they can in this winter wet."

Grizzl was small and slight of build, her face brown from the sun and wrinkled, her teeth all gone or mostly so. Although her arms were strong and well muscled from the lifting and wringing of wet linen, her wrists and elbows were swollen and bruised and red.

Matilda watched Grizzl, coughing again, struggle to lift the mass of soggy linen. The girl bent to help her, fearing that Grizzl would perish before she ever finished and Peg would be angered. While Horanswith Leech waited within, Grizzl and Matilda hung wet laundry from bushes, fence posts, and the thatch of the cottage roof. Matilda's hands froze, her clothes dripped icy drips, and her back ached. Never at the manor had she thought of who did the laundry. She hoped it was not a tiny hobbled woman like Grizzl.

Finally they entered Grizzl's cottage. It was dark and smoky. More laundry had been hung about the room, carefully, so it did not drag on the dirt floor or hang in the small fire pit. Grizzl had no table, no bench, no bedstead, only a small straw mattress where she sat herself down now. While Horanswith Leech felt her pulse, Arelda, Agrippina, Gerty, and the other leeches fed on her blood, until, swollen and satiated, they dropped off.

Matilda was speechless with horror, but Leech seemed pleased and Grizzl content.

"Good work," said Leech, "my beauties, my hungry swarm. Did that make your tiny bellies warm?" He caressed each leech as he dropped it back into the leather pouch. He took the small coin Grizzl offered, frowned at it and then shrugged, put his bleeding bowl back on his head, and bowed to Matilda. "I trust you can find your way back without me leading? I must be about my bleeding." Matilda assured him she could, and he left.

She warmed her hands at the ruins of the tiny fire, as Peg had showed her, before rubbing Grizzl's joints with liniment. At first Matilda felt timid about putting her hands to Grizzl's arms and shoulders, but soon she settled into the work, and the rhythm soothed her as well as Grizzl.

"I knew Peg had someone to help her," Grizzl said as she gave Matilda a farthing in payment, "but I didn't know she would be so pretty."

"Father Leufredus always called it a pity if all one had to be proud of was being pretty." Matilda shook her head violently. Obviously Horanswith Leech's way of speaking had corrupted her mind. She quickly wiped her hands on her skirt, nodded farewell, and left Grizzl's house.

Matilda walked slowly back along the river. Although the water smelled of fish and garbage, a cold but fresh wind that blew from the meadows across the river brought the scent of growing things.

Along the riverbank the proprietors of cook shops tempted with all manner of fine foods: "Bread with butter, ale and wine, ribs of beef both fat and fine." She could have roast snipe for a penny, or ten roast finches, or a leg of rabbit, but did not have a penny, only the farthing that really belonged to Peg. Still, smells were free, so she went from stall to stall enjoying the hot and pungent odors.

Finally she turned back toward the center of town. The high walls of great houses, enormous gray steeples, and stone towers glittered against the sky. Next to them were weedy patches of ground and hovels no better than Grizzl's tiny cottage. Matilda knew the poor must be poor by God's will, but how did He decide, she wondered, who would live in a great house and who in a cottage? It would be simpler if the good were rich and the evil doomed to poverty, but she knew it was not that easy.

Stopping before one cottage in such ruin that it appeared to stand only through sheer stubbornness, she thought, *I could have landed somewhere even more wretched than Peg's shop. I could live here and be but laundress's helper or bloodletter's girl or apprentice plucker of chickens.* Lost in thought as she was, Matilda was not surprised to discover that she had also lost her way. She did not mind. The wandering gave her time useful for thinking.

"Thank Saint Gobnet you are back," said Peg when Matilda returned and handed her Grizzl's farthing. "Else I would have had to grow another hand. Andrew Potter here has broken his wrist. Mix this plaster for a splint."

Matilda took the pot and a wooden ladle and began to mix the plaster. Perhaps, she thought as she stirred, she should be somewhat grateful and try harder to please Mistress Peg so she would not be sent somewhere worse, somewhere where Father Leufredus would never find her. Somewhere like the dungeon where Saint Agnes was confined before being led naked through the streets of—

"Matilda!" shouted Peg, grabbing the pot from the girl. "You have let the plaster dry! It is now as useless as you are. What have you been about?"

"I was remembering Saint—"

"Forget your saints for a moment! You must learn to attend to what and where you are right now, or you are no use to me. Heaven will wait for you." She began to pound and pry the dry plaster to free it from the pot. "See what has happened? Did you not think?"

"I did not know it would grow so stiff," Matilda said in a voice as stiff as the plaster.

"Think about what you are doing. And if you do not know, ask. I know this work is strange to you. Do you not have questions?"

Matilda shook her head.

"Not one? Not why or how or what will happen if?"

"Father Leufredus said curiosity revealed an unquiet mind. He preferred I just listen and obey."

"Well, I thank God and His holy mother every day that I am not Father Leufredus. Me you may ask if you want to learn."

Matilda was not sure she wanted to learn and not at all thankful that Peg was not Father Leufredus. She said only, "I will do as you bid me."

As days passed, Matilda busied herself boiling, bandaging, and bonesetting. She grew better at paying attention, mixing plasters, wrapping limbs, and restraining struggling patients. She assisted in setting broken wrists, sprained ankles, and wrenched necks. She pounded comfrey into juicy pulp, drained it through linen cloth, and packed it across straightened bones to dry and stiffen. As the winter went on, they did brisk business in broken hands and fractured jaws, for ale was cheap and tempers short. Women lifted loads far too heavy and wrenched backs, knees, and necks. Men slipped on the ice and needed to have their ribs bandaged.

Soon enough it seemed to Matilda that her whole world had become sore knees, cracked ribs, stiffened elbows, and arthritic joints in the jaw, the shoulder, and the toes. Sometimes the pounding on the wooden door signaled fish or bread peddlers hawking their wares house to house, or street sellers with pepper and garlic, but most often it was someone needing Peg's help.

Peg offered Matilda companionship, sausages, and an occasional bout of draughts, but the girl refused it all and felt as alone as the moon. She did not belong here. She wished to devote herself to holy words and higher things. What was such a one doing on Blood and Bone Alley? *Dear Saint Ursula,* she prayed, *martyred with your eleven thousand companions, have pity on me who am all alone.* Saint Ursula answered, *Eleven thousand companions can be very trying at times. How I wished to be alone now and then.*

Still, oh, how Matilda longed for Father Leufredus, for a life that did not plague her with questions and uncertainty. But Father Leufredus did not return. And still the winter went on.

CHAPTER SEVEN

Finding Another Matilda

 "Here," said Peg to Matilda, handing her five pennies. "This is for the butcher and the baker. And these," she said, adding another two to the pile in Matilda's hand, "are for you. You have earned them."

Matilda stared at the coins in her hand. She'd earned them. Never before had she owned any money, for at the manor she was given what she needed. The coins appeared to shine in the dimness of the room. Matilda bobbed her head in thanks to Peg and hurried back to the buttery. There was a small sky-blue jug on the lowest shelf. She dropped her two pennies into the jug, satisfied at their clink and clank. She had earned them! She turned and ran off to the market.

It was a rare fair day. The pale sun shone feebly in the blue sky. Peg's instructions still sounded in

Matilda's ears: "Get a bit of bacon, three eggs (pay no more than a ha'penny for them), beef bones with some meat still on them and not all fat, a cabbage (green and firm with no worms), the freshest bread the thieving baker has, and a penny's worth of tallow candles." She chose to walk a new way and get lost, for she had thinking to do. Nearly two months had passed, and Father Leufredus had neither returned from London nor sent for her. What did that mean?

Turning an unfamiliar corner, she beheld a magnificent house, the finest she had seen but for the goldsmiths' guild hall and the Lord Mayor's residence. Tall wooden gates faced the street, open now to reveal a cobbled forecourt, stream, stable, and garden. As Matilda stood and admired, a young girl with dark hair and a lively step came through the gates.

"Matilda!" someone shouted from the house. "Matilda, you ninny! You backside of a donkey!"

Matilda jumped. Who was calling her in such a way?

"Yes, Mistress Annet. I'm here," replied the dark-haired girl.

"Do you have the coins? How are you going to buy whitefish without the coins?"

"I have them right here!" The girl jingled the pouch at her belt. "Someday," she said as she passed

Matilda, "there will be one insult too many and I will be gone. Or Fat Annet there will be found with her throat slit."

Matilda was intrigued by this fierce girl from the fine house. She asked, "Your name is Matilda?"

The girl nodded. "Mostly they call me Tildy, when they're not angry with me. I am the kitchen maid."

"I am Matilda also," said Matilda.

Tildy smiled as brightly as a full moon. "Two Matildas! It must be God's plan that we be friends."

Matilda thought God had better things to concern Himself with than a kitchen maid's friendships, but still she walked with the girl toward the market square, examining her as they went. Tildy was of middling height, with small waist and broad hips. Under her nut-brown hair were curious black eyes in a thin, dark face with the slight look of a rodent. For all that, Matilda thought her not unlovely, although not at all meek or obedient or holy.

"Mistress Annet Greedyguts is nought but the housekeeper," said Tildy, "although she thinks she owns the house and all in it. She hates me because I am not content to be in the kitchen." She smiled. "Someday I will be a lady's maid and comb my lady's hair, stiffen the pleats on her best wimple, and brush the crumbs from her velvet mantle. I have had enough of kitchens. Look at my hands!" Tildy held up her hands, red, peeling, and cracked.

"Is there a lady in the house?" asked Matilda.

"Yes, but she has old Elsa, who does for her. And there is no one else but Master Theobald. Still, I will find a great lady somewhere someday who will have me." Her lips were firm and tight, her chin set. Matilda had no doubt she could do what she said.

"This Theobald. Is he the master physician?"

"Master Theobald is indeed a physician. A healer and a wonderworker," said Tildy.

"I saw him once in the street," said Matilda. "He seemed clever and learned. Would that I could attend to such as him instead of Mistress Peg."

"Indeed, I am learning much just by living in his house," Tildy said. "Not about physicking but about fine houses and fine clothes and fine food. But I cannot let Fat Annet catch me out of the kitchen. The witch."

They passed a man walking a goose on a string. Matilda stared, thinking them perhaps entertainers on their way to the market square. But Tildy said, "That is Samson. He's taking a goose to the kitchen of the inn. Take care not to walk behind them, geese being notorious despoilers of the street. And there is Mary Weaversgirl, the silk spinner. She must be on her way to sell her silk to Master Orron. Oh, look, she sees Lucy Goode, the rosary maker. They do not speak. See how they just nod stiffly."

"Watch out . . ." "There goes . . ." "See . . ." As they walked, Tildy continued pointing out people and places Matilda had never before noticed. Tildy seemed to know everyone and was interested in everything. Matilda felt she was seeing the town with new eyes.

Reaching the Shambles, they passed the butchers' stalls with their skinned carcasses of rabbit, lamb, and (some said) cat, hanging from poles, heads lolling, mouths open. The sight always made Matilda shudder delightfully, as if they were tiny martyrs. Today they reminded her of Hag. Never before had she met a cursed cat with a name. Hag. She felt a stab of pity and did not like it.

"I made a good bargain for the fish and have a farthing left over for a raisin pie," said Tildy. "Will you share it?"

Matilda was silent. Would Father Leufredus wish her to be friendly to this girl? Surely not. But Tildy's invitation made Matilda feel surprisingly warm within, so she accepted.

The girls ate sitting on the edge of the wide stone basin surrounding the bubbling spring that served as the town well. The women of the town were drenching their dirty linen in the icy water and slapping it mightily against the stones. Matilda watched the laughing, chattering women with their sleeves rolled up to reveal strong, red arms, skirts pulled high, feet bare to spare their shoes. They gossiped as they washed: Helga of Baywater Village had given birth to a baby who was half wolf and half snake; Samuel Fuller's bad skin cleared right up after he set fire to a toadskin at midnight; Gilbert Carpenter was cured of fever by the great Theobald (Tildy nudged Matilda and smiled), who had prescribed eating only cooling foods: grapes, woodcock broth, kid's foot jelly.

Matilda heard a familiar name: "Old Mother Uffa," said a young woman kneeling in the water and scrubbing, "from Blood and Bone Alley has finally died. Her son claims it is because she spit into his cook fire, but I think she finally ran out of days. Her house has been rented. Some say to a witch."

Matilda told Tildy, "I can imagine what Peg will say when she hears this news: 'Witch or no, I do hope she plays draughts.'"

Tildy laughed a morsel of the raisin pie right out of her mouth. Matilda was surprised. She had not meant to be funny, but Tildy's laughter was so infectious, Matilda might have joined her had she not thought what Father Leufredus would say about such foolishness—her laughing and gossiping with a kitchen maid, unlettered and unholy, and enjoying it. Matilda jumped down from the well and said, "I should not be here laughing."

"Why not?"

"It would be better for me to spend the time in prayer."

"I myself think laughing is mighty like praying," said Tildy, "as if saying 'Listen, God, how much I enjoy this world You have made.'"

This sounded much like blasphemy. "I must go."

"Please come again someday. I know God meant for us two Matildas to find each other. Maybe someday we could get a place together. I would be a lady's maid, and you . . . what can you do?"

"I have reading and writing in Latin and a bit in French," Matilda said. "I know the Ten Commandments, the seven moral virtues, and the fourteen articles of the faith. I know which saint to invoke against oversleeping and which to call upon when in peril at sea, and I can quote Augustine of Canterbury on Saint Gregory the Great and Saint Gregory on Augustine. I can recite in Greek about the meaning of free will and whether God can be seen in his essence and—"

"Gor," said Tildy. "But what can you *do*?"

"I am attendant to Red Peg the Bonesetter," said Matilda, "but I hope to be leaving her soon."

"And where is it you would go?"

"Somewhere, anywhere, with Father Leufredus."
Matilda sighed. "But right now I must go back to
Mistress Peg's. She will be waiting."

"Don't forget me," Tildy called.

Matilda thought she would not forget Tildy, with
her bright eyes and laughter and blasphemous notions.
Laughing like praying—what an idea! As if God wanted
us to enjoy this world! Matilda shook her head.

As she completed her tasks, she mourned once
again for her old life. She saw in her mind Father
Leufredus leading prayers in the manor chapel with
light from the colored windows shining on his face,
Father Leufredus reading from the Life of Saint James
the Dismembered, Father Leufredus lecturing in Latin
on evil, sin, devils, Hell, and eternal lakes of fire.
Matilda sighed a very big sigh, remembering the days
when she was uninvolved in all the matters of the
world, of pain and illness, of unsuitable friends and
useless skills. It was easier at the manor, where the
most difficult thing she did was walk to the privy in
winter.

CHAPTER EIGHT

Watching Tom

 One Friday when Matilda returned to Peg's from the market, there were Doctor Margery, Grizzl Wimplewasher, and Juliana Parchmenter. "See who has come for draughts and a bite of supper," Peg said. "Come and join us."

The shop looked cozy, with Grizzl at the table pouring ale, Doctor Margery complaining, Peg toasting oatcakes by the fire. Father Leufredus would spurn such company, but Matilda's heart longed for friends of her own.

"Here, Matilda," said Juliana, setting up the draughts board, "I will show you the secrets and mysteries of this most splendid game."

"She will not," said Peg, "for the girl seeks higher things."

"Such as ladders?" asked Juliana. "Or the moon?"

"Or roof thatch?" added Grizzl.

"No. Such as those early apples just out of reach on the treetops," said Peg, and they all laughed.

Matilda flushed red. They were taunting her, she thought—a bonesetter, a laundress, a merchant, and a goose girl. Matilda pulled herself closer to the fire and thought about all the ways in which she was worthier than they.

Grizzl's laughter turned into furious coughing. "Pardon our jesting," she said when she was able. "I am most pleased to see you again. How well you look. Even the fire is dimmed by your pink and pretty face."

"I so long to be frail and pale like the holy saints," Matilda told her, "but instead I *would* have these rosy cheeks."

"Frail and pale, my elbow!" shouted Doctor Margery. "This you say to Grizzl, who has seen six babies and a husband waste away, frail and pale, in that poor house by the river where the dampness never leaves your bones! You are fortunate to have Peg's good food and dry house, a strong constitution, and those rosy cheeks."

Matilda wiped bits of Margery's oatcake off her sleeve and gritted her teeth so she would not shout back. Almost she could hear Father Leufredus saying, "Meek and obedient, Matilda, meek and obedient.

into sin."

Peg took Margery by the arm and said, "Joints that have not been used grow frozen and stiff. The same might be said of a young girl's heart. I suppose we must be more patient, Marg."

Matilda was shocked at the hearing. Her heart frozen and stiff? Her heart that was warm with loneliness and soft with longing? How little they knew her here.

She moved to the door and threw it open, hoping to escape from these women, but she was stopped by a hubble-bubble outside. A small, hairy man, in mustard-colored tunic and green hose, was trying to persuade an ox to pull a very large wagon through the very narrow alley. "*Ite,*" he shouted. "*Ite, bestia diabolus. Ad supplicium aeternum damno!*"

Latin! It was cursing, but it was Latin! Perhaps the man was a lawyer or a university master or a great physician from Paris or Salerno. Or a saintly priest. Matilda stared at him.

Peg pushed her out of the doorway. "Tom!" she cried, enfolding the man in her great embrace, lifting him right up so that Matilda could see nothing of him but his hairy hands about Peg's neck. There was much hugging and kissing and pounding of backs and shoulders. When

Peg set him down and moved aside, Matilda could see he had the widest shoulders she had ever seen. And the shortest legs. And the biggest nose, which was so like a turnip, it put her in mind of supper. His little raisin eyes peered out under grizzled brows in a face as writhled and brown as a beef roast, and he smiled a great, merry smile. So this was Peg's Tom. He didn't look particularly wise and learned, but he was speaking Latin. Matilda waited eagerly to hear what he would say.

"My old Peg. I am as happy to see you as sweet ale in summer," he said as he pulled a lock of carrot-red hair from under her kerchief. "And Grizzl and Juliana. Are ye still here or here again?"

After much laughter he turned to Margery. "How goes the physicking business, Doctor Marg?"

"Breeding and bleeding. My business is all breeding and bleeding—they breed and I bleed them." And there was more laughter.

Finally he noticed Matilda. "Do I see a new face?"

"Indeed," said Peg. "This is my helper, Matilda, who seeks higher things."

"*Ave, doctissime*," said Matilda, greeting with a slight curtsy the most learned man.

"Can she not talk right, pretty Peg?" the man asked with a worried frown. "Perhaps I have something in my wagon to heal—"

Was he jesting with her? "It was Latin, sir. I heard you speaking it to your ox."

"Oh, Saint Brendan there. He used to belong to a priest, and those are the only words will make him go. I am not much for Latin."

No Latin. "But Mistress Peg says you are a man of learning."

"Well, I know where to find mistletoe, why spotted lizard cures stomach ills, and how to brew a wood betony tea for banishing monstrous nocturnal visions. Of course," he said with a wink, "too much wood betony can also *cause* monstrous nocturnal visions. Depends on who is paying."

Matilda was speechless. This was Peg's man of learning? No Latin, no medicine, just mistletoe and spotted lizard?

That night, as Matilda lay on her pallet in the buttery, she could hear Peg's and Tom's voices as they played a game of draughts, talking over the day and laughing. She felt a rush of loneliness.

The next morning Peg fixed up a place for Tom to work at one end of the table. *How long will he be here?* Matilda wondered. *Will Mistress Peg still need me?* If Peg had no use for her and turned her out, where would she go?

Matilda kept one eye and one ear on Tom as she

pounded and pulled and boiled. "'Tis but a rash," he said to Milo the Pepperer. "Rub some of this salve on your neck and spit three times in the moonlight."

To Roger Smith, "Here are pieces of dried dragon fat to sprinkle on your food to soothe and heal your stomach," and to Juliana Parchmenter, who had brought her unhappy daughter-in-law, "I recommend a tea of moonwort berries for wounds, poisons, and such as are become peevish."

Tom took a great deal of time with each, talking and listening, trading jokes and passing on gossip, asking about this one's mother and that one's baby daughter and even an occasional pig or ox. Weepy children always found raisins in a dirty leather bag at his belt. Tom was never without his raisin bag.

On Thursday came young William Baker with a dog bite on his leg. Tom spread a potion of mustard and club moss on it, but the boy cried with the sting and tried to wipe it off. Tom said nothing but took from his leather bag an apple, which he proceeded to peel, the peel falling from the apple in one long, snaky spiral. Longer and longer the strip of peel got. Matilda stared fascinated, everything else forgotten as she waited for the peel to grow longer still or to break. And she saw William Baker doing the same, mindless of his pain as he watched.

Amazingly, the peel never did break. Tom took the snake, wrapped it about his neck, and cut the apple into pieces for a less tearful William.

Next a young woman came from a neighboring village for a love potion, which Tom supplied with a wink. "Love potion?" asked Matilda after the woman left. "You will be sent to Hell with the witches and devils."

"There be no such thing as love potions," said Tom. "That were just elderberries and a rotten egg. But if she uses it, she will think he loves her, and so will act as if he loves her. They will walk hand in hand by the river, which runs silver in the moonlight, and by cock's crow he will think he loves her too."

Matilda merely sniffed.

One morning, with Peg gone to Grizzl's, Matilda burned the porridge. "Here," said Tom, after he showed Gilbert Carpenter out, "let me scrub that well for you, and you buy more porridge, and Peg will never know." He winked at her. "'Tis not deception, but defense."

While he scoured the pot with pewterwort stems, Matilda said, "I hope porridge costs no more than a ha'penny, for then I might have enough left for more parchment. For writing," she said at his blank look.

"I never did see much purpose in this writing," he said.

"Why, all learned people can write. I write letters to Father Leufredus, who is far away. Scholars like Father Leufredus write of the lives of the saints or devotions. Or folk in business keep records and accounts."

"Like what?"

"Well, if I were to keep your accounts, you would know how many bottles of moonwort tea and pots of mistletoe salve you made and sold and for how much, how many stomachs were soothed and how many heads, which towns paid better prices for which remedies."

"And why would I want to know that?"

"Why, to know."

"But such an account book wouldn't tell the important things I know," Tom said. "Who is getting married to whom and where the bridal ale will be, where to find the best mules or lumber for the lowest price, who in Giggleswick is the best man to see for a new axle or oats or a quick pint, who prefers singing and joking when his tooth is pulled and who likes silence, where to pound a baby's back so she stops her fearful fretting and finally belches." He finished scrubbing the pot, dipped it into the bucket of water near the fire to rinse, and dried it by swinging it above his head. "All that writing you do and still you know only 'so many' and 'how much.'"

Such things might be important to Tom, but Father Leufredus would not think much of them. Matilda shook her head in disappointment.

Tom left again on a morning so cold that he had to wrap Saint Brendan's snout in rags to keep his hot breath from freezing. The sound of rumbling cart and mumbled Latin sounded on the air long after Tom and the ox turned the corner and were out of sight.

I am happy he has gone, Matilda thought. *He is no man of learning but instead a fraud.* To her horror, she found that she had not thought those words, but had spoken them aloud. And Peg had heard them. Matilda looked at Peg's raised eyebrows and hurriedly stammered, "Oh, forgive me, Mistress Peg. I did not mean to speak aloud. . . . I mean, I would not . . ."

Peg quieted her with a wave. "Speak up, Matilda. Why do you think Tom a fraud?"

Matilda whispered, "How can—"

"Louder," said Peg.

Matilda cleared her throat and began again. "How can he be a great man of learning if he has no Latin or reading or writing and knows only rotten eggs, apple peels, and spotted lizard?" She stopped and waited to be punished for finding fault with Tom or at least failing in meekness.

"There are different kinds of learning. Tom knows

many things," Peg said, "even if it is true that more visit him to be delivered of elf shot or evil dreams than boils, spots, or other bodily ailments. He has a way with him, never too busy to talk or too tired to listen. Those who come go away satisfied, eagerly awaiting his next visit. Do you think that is worth nothing?"

Matilda breathed deeply in her relief that Peg was not angry with her. "No," she said. "In truth I myself have seen him give comfort and hope to people. But Father Leufredus—"

"Bah. Enough of what Father Leufredus thinks. Let us talk more about this when you know what Matilda thinks."

Matilda pondered this as she huddled close to the brazier that night, it being too cold for her pallet in a room without a fire. How, she thought as she took off her boots, could Peg not see Tom truly? Was his nature not apparent to all who looked? How could Matilda see a different Tom from the one Peg saw? And how could Peg see things one way and Father Leufredus another? Did this not mean Peg was wrong?

She stood up, quickly jerked her kirtle off, and wrapped herself in her thin quilt. Sitting down cross-legged before the fire again, she warmed her hands. Why did everyone not see things as she and Father Leufredus did? And why, despite her doubts in Tom, did she have the nagging feeling that Tom knew much that she did not know, things she did not even know she did not know?

There were more questions in this world, Matilda thought, even than the number of fleas St. Finnian of Clonard drove out of the Isle of Flatholm. And for most of them there seemed to be no answers.

Meeting Walter and Nathaniel

 Peg said, "Take these four pennies and go to Ralph Thwirp the tanner, the Devil take him for his high prices. We need more ox hides for splints."

The morning was cold but clear as Matilda set off for the tanner's yard by the river. The sun was melting the snow and thawing the piles of refuse in the street. For a while she walked behind Master Theobald and a woman Matilda took to be his wife. She walked serenely at her husband's side, nodding to those he nodded to, smiling at those he smiled at, head cocked to hear his every word.

That could be me with Father Leufredus, Matilda thought with envy. And she watched until they turned away and even their footsteps disappeared with the melting snow.

Still thinking about Father Leufredus, Matilda slipped on the icy slush, tripped over something, and fell hard onto her rump. The something proved itself a black-haired boy, sitting with eyes closed at the side of the street.

Slowly he opened his eyes, as round and brown as currant buns. His face radiated common sense, good humor, and a mockery that Matilda found irritating and most unholy.

The irritation, the sting in her bottom, and the hot red scrapes on her palms loosened Matilda's tongue. "*Fungus! Porcus! Stultus!* No, *stultissimus!* You, stupidest of all boys, should be seized for assault," she said sharply as she picked herself up and brushed muck off her skirts.

"And you, my girl, for daytime dreaming and not watching where you are going," he said.

"*Me?* But *you* were sitting on the street with your face to the sky, not watching to see whose way you were in."

The boy shrugged. "My master told me I was looking too pale and sent me out for some sun. My master is the apothecary there," he said, gesturing toward the large shop behind him, "and I am his apprentice, Walter At-Water, though some call me Walter Mudd for the muddy salves and plasters smeared on my tunic."

"It is a fitting name for you, for never have I seen a boy so dirty."

"Nor I a girl so small, with eyes as green as grass, cheeks like peaches, and hair as gold as an ouzel's belly."

Matilda stared at him. Her cheeks grew warm. "Appearance counts for nothing, as the body is but a vessel for the soul, which should be meek and humble. . . ."

"Then might I say, 'Never have I seen a girl with such comely humility'? Or perhaps 'I am overawed by your undistinguished, humble-spirited, humble-minded, humble-hearted, humble-looking humility, which humbly shines . . .'?"

As Matilda opened her mouth to reply, he stood up, bowed to her, and said, "We shall meet again. The glow from your triumphant humility will lead me to wherever you are. Also your green eyes."

The boy called Walter Mudd then winked at her and strode off whistling toward the shop.

Matilda frowned at his back. "*Stultissimus!*" she whispered. "He is as irritating as a pebble in the boot." She pulled a strand of hair across her shoulder and looked at it closely. Like an ouzel's belly, he had said. What, she thought, might an ouzel be? *Piscis aut avis? Lepus aut leo?* Fish or bird? Rabbit or lion? Whichever, it had a belly as gold as her hair, and she almost smiled as she continued on to Ralph Thwirp the tanner, the Devil take him.

Soon it was the Day of Ashes, the first day of Lent. Matilda awoke before dawn, disturbed by the sound of the church bells, which clunked rather than rang, it being that cold. Sticking a bare foot outside the quilt, she gasped at the chill and pulled her toes in again, snuggling down in the Matilda-shaped warm space in the hard straw mattress.

Finally she jumped up, naked as a needle, pulled on her shift and kirtle, and danced across the icy floor into the front room. "You look cold as a frog," called Peg from her bed.

An eel, a flea, and now a frog, thought Matilda. Did Peg even know she was a human being, made in God's image? Matilda stirred the ashes remaining in the iron brazier, blew on the embers, added kindling, and said a prayer to Saint Florian that the fire would start easily this time. It did; she was growing better at fires.

The church bells tolled for Mass. "Are you not going to Mass on this holy day?" Matilda asked Peg, who had not yet stuck foot out from under cover.

Peg shook her head. "Heaven is but a promise, while a warm bed is right now. I shall pray from here." Matilda thought it must be much easier not to be holy and obedient on a morning as cold as this.

She wrapped herself in her cloak—still damp from yesterday, for nothing dried in this cold—and hurried to the church. An icy rain was falling, and the sharp wind tugged at her cloak as if trying to pull it from her. Father Leufredus said the wind was the whistling of the Devil. Matilda shuddered, only partly from cold. She could hear the demon coming around corners and hiding in small spaces, and she crossed herself as she hurried to the safety of the church.

Although not crowded even on this holy morning, still the church was noisy with the sound of talking, scratching, and coughing. Feet shuffled on frozen rushes and stamped on the floor for warmth. But the gleam of the candles on silver and gold, the starchy smell of the linen and vestments, and the cloud of fragrant incense in the air promised what Heaven would be like. Mass made Matilda feel as if God were right there in church with her, even if she couldn't see Him. Most people looked about or gossiped or slept through Mass, but Matilda listened carefully, for sometimes amid the mumbling of the priest she could catch a word or two of Latin.

Matilda especially loved the Day of Ashes, for the priest dipped his thumb in holy ashes and marked the foreheads of the churchgoers: *"Pulvis es,"* you are dust. Matilda knew the ashes were supposed to be a reminder of mortality, but to her the smudge felt like a mark of holiness, as if those who saw her would know that although but an attendant to a bonesetter, she was marked for God and Heaven. On her way back to Peg's she felt her forehead again and again to make sure the ashes were still there.

On the Saturday after, when Gregory Merchantson paid Peg with a fish pie only two days old for setting his broken arm, Peg invited Margery and Nathaniel Cross, the apothecary, to dine.

First she set aside a mighty slice of the pie for Nathaniel to take back to his wife, Sarah, who could not easily leave their shop. Then she set the other slices on the scrubbed table for herself and Margery on one side, and Matilda and Nathaniel on the other.

It was Matilda's first opportunity to meet Nathaniel Cross. She was curious to see the man whom Peg spoke of as the best soul God ever made. Was he saintly and wise? Or no more a great man than Tom was?

What he was was straight as a stick and small as an elf, with a bald, freckled head and eyes that surprised her with their blueness. Blue as the Virgin's veil, they were, blue as the summer sky.

Chewing on a slice of hard bread, for thank God his teeth were still good, Nathaniel talked softly to them of his troubles. He had long been shortsighted, he said, but now his eyesight had weakened so that he could no longer see clearly what was right before his face. "The guild master has heard about my failing sight," Nathaniel said. "He knows of my slowness and mistakes."

He stopped. Peg stood and patted his shoulder, and he continued, "I told him it were true and he ordered me, with affection and pity but ordered me nonetheless, to cease practicing by summer. 'An apothecary,' he said, 'who can't be trusted to tell angelica from almond oil is no apothecary at all.'" As he said this, Nathaniel's eyes filled with hopeless tears.

Matilda was moved at the sight of those blue eyes overflowing with sorrow. "Father Leufredus says God uses illness and disease to punish the wicked. Perhaps if you were to repent?" she asked softly.

Margery stood up so quickly the bench fell over. "You ungracious, thoughtless, ill-mannered girl! You think Nathaniel's eye troubles stem from *wickedness*? Why, Nathaniel is . . . is . . . is . . ."

Matilda stood also. She had suffered enough from this goose girl, but before she could respond, Nathaniel reached over and touched Margery's arm. "She was speaking to me, Margery. Let me answer her." Margery hauled the bench upright and sat back down with a thud, and Nathaniel turned toward Matilda, motioning her to sit as well. Matilda did so, grateful that Nathaniel had saved her from the temptation to speak her mind to Margery.

"It would be easier if I *were* wicked," Nathaniel said, "for repentance is well within my abilities. But unhappily I am no thief, no murderer, no traitor or seducer of women. I do not commune with devils or magicians. I am just an old man, young Matilda, and no better and no worse than any other man, not perfect but not wicked. I am an apothecary. I know and love herbs and healing. I can do nothing else, and I do not wish to." He snuffled, wiping his eyes on his sleeve.

Matilda could think of nothing to say to that. Glowering at Margery, for her anger was merely stifled and not forgotten, she took another bite of her pie.

"Would a wee bout of draughts comfort you, Nathaniel?" Peg asked, drawing her red eyebrows together in consternation.

Nathaniel shook his head. "No, thank ye, Peg. Not at the moment. I can think about little but my bad eyes. I saw Leech the bloodletter, but the bites of his leeches festered." Matilda was not at all surprised. "Walter had to anoint them with powdered larch bark and egg white. And my eyes are no better. Peter Threadneedle told me how the worm doctor had destroyed the worm that was paining his tooth. I thought perhaps he could help me, too." Nathaniel shook his head. "He could do nothing, and indeed, two days later, Peter himself betook his throbbing tooth to Barber Slodge to have it pulled. So desperate am I that I too stopped to see the barbers."

Boggle and Slodge were Blood and Bone Alley's barber-surgeons, who would cut your hair, your whiskers, or your leg off if you had the coin, for the alley was too poor a place to attract the kind of surgeon who does not also cut hair. Matilda knew their shop by the buckets of blood and bloody rags outside but had never been within.

"The barbers?" she asked. "Were you not afeared? Did you have to watch them cut off someone's leg?"

Nathaniel smiled and answered, "No, no. Indeed, much of their business is but tending dog bites, pulling teeth, and trimming beards."

"Were they any help with your eyes?" asked Peg.

"Boggle said obviously I want vomiting. Never, said Slodge, just a good cleanout of my bowels. 'Foul fiend!' Boggle shouted. 'Would you kill the man?' When they began talking about boiling oil, blistering, and excisions, I left the shop in a hurry."

Margery, Peg, and Nathaniel all laughed. The noise finally slowed to a wheeze and a sneeze, and Peg said, "Poor Nathaniel, is there no help for you? My mother used to say there was nothing like cabbage and honey to improve eyesight, though do you eat it or spread it on, I do not know. Or onion juice in the eye, or the blood of a tortoise, or seed of wild cucumber crushed in water, or—"

"Superstitions," said Doctor Margery. "Useless superstitions. Medicine teaches us that the eyes send unseen visual rays out to an object. If these rays are disturbed—by wine, women, baths, leeks or onions, by garlic, mustard seed, fire, light or smoke, dust, pepper, or beans—the sight fails."

The goose girl's opinions? Surely Nathaniel would laugh at her, but to Matilda's surprise he asked, "This then is what ails me?"

Margery shrugged. "It could also be a test from God, some foreign substance in the eye, or a cancer in the brain. Most likely it is because you are old, Nathaniel, and your eyes are wearing out like the soles of your shoes."

Master Nathaniel sat silent.

Matilda imagined his eyes fading from summer-sky blue to gray and misting over with blindness. She felt sadness, and the feeling frightened her. It was the sign of an earthly attachment. Father Leufredus would surely disapprove. Still, there it was, sadness, and another feeling she did not recognize. The nameless feeling tightened her chest, tickled her throat, and made her long to touch Nathaniel gently, the way Peg did. She thought of all the words that might describe this new feeling—compassion, pity, sympathy, mercy—but decided it was best said in Latin: *misericordia*, distress of the heart.

CHAPTER TEN

Doing her Best

Lightning split the sky, followed by a great clap of thunder and a torrent of soft raindrops. There was a sweet smell in the air. Spring was but a promise, but a promise was better than winter.

Matilda was alone, Peg off seeing to Grizzl, when a man came seeking Peg, his right hand cradled in his left, pain in his eyes. Stephen Bybridge, for that is what he was called, living as he did near the bridge to the eastern part of town, said, "My hand aches some'ut fierce and prickles run up and down my arm, like bugs was dancin' on it, but I can see no bugs. Might Mistress Peg know what is wrong?"

"Mistress Peg is from home," Matilda said. She was about to bid him come another day when she thought, *I have learned well from Father Leufredus. Surely with his knowledge I can be useful.*

To Stephen Bybridge she, eager yet a bit apprehensive, said again, "Mistress Peg is from home, but *I* will do what I can."

She prayed silently to saints known to listen favorably to petitions from the faithful. She recalled the Latin words for hand (*manus*), arm (*brachium*), pain (*dolor*), even bugs (*formicae*—well, truly that was ants, but was the closest Matilda could come at the moment). She tried to remember what Thomas Aquinas and Saint Augustine might have said about hands and arms, but recalled only texts about resting in the hands of God. Comforting, but no help for Stephen Bybridge.

She thought of the saints in Heaven who suffered withered arms, useless arms, missing arms. Were they cured? How? Was any saint ever cured of an aching hand? She could not think of one. She could think of no saint with bugs or prickles on his arm, although Saint Mark was said to be effective against fly bites. Disheartened, she admitted that what she had learned from Father Leufredus was no help here. She gave up trying her learning and her Latin. She would try what she had learned so far from Peg.

Carefully she examined Stephen's hand, his arm, his elbow. She felt his forehead. Very gently, she moved his hand around. Then she looked at him, sat back, looked at the ceiling, and looked at him again.

"I do not know what to do now," she admitted. "I do not know. Best you wait for Mistress Peg."

Soon enough Mistress Peg arrived. "I tried to help him, Mistress Peg," said Matilda. "I tried everything I know but could not." She shook her head sadly.

"Knowing is not enough. You must also listen and look," said Peg, hanging her cloak on its hook. "What did you ask him?" Matilda was silent. "Well, look at him. What do you see?"

"I see an oldish man in a dusty tunic and worn boots of hard leather, with brown hair, a hopeful face, and a hand that pains him."

"Let me see what *I* can see," Peg said. She examined the man's arm. "Has this arm ever been broken?" she asked him.

"No," he said.

"The wrist? Any of the fingers? The thumb?"

He shook his head.

"Have you suffered a severe blow to the elbow?"

"No," he said again.

"I am puzzled as to just what is wrong and why."

Matilda felt less stupid; Peg did not know what to do either. But where did that leave poor Stephen Bybridge?

"Please, mistress," he said, "do what you can. If I

can't work, I can't eat. And no more can my little ones."

"Tell me," Peg said to Stephen, "how long has it pained you?"

"Since Saturday."

"Tell me everything you did Saturday."

"I woke with the bells, washed me hands and ears. Had a bit of bread and ale. Gathered me tools and went over to the priory, where we are building a tower. Gregory Haresfoot was there already, so I picked up me chisel and—"

"Your chisel?" Peg asked loudly. "What work is it you do?"

"I am a stonemason, and a fine one, in truth. Leastwise I was . . ."

"Thundering toads!" Peg shouted. "I know what's amiss." Matilda moved in to watch as Peg moved Stephen's hand this way and that, bent it and pulled it, asked, "Does this hurt?" and "How is this?" and "This?"

She sat back and smiled. "I've seen this before in a mason. The joint here where your thumb meets your wrist is sprained from the pounding and jarring of heavy hammers on chisels. I can splint it. You rest it, and you'll be sound as a bell in no time." Peg took Stephen's hand. "Matilda, bring me the ash-bark ointment and soak a strip of that leather in water. No. A smaller strip. There. Yes, like that."

Matilda wondered how it would feel to save someone's hand or his livelihood or his life. Father Leufredus thought theology more important than medicine, but Matilda could not think how theology could have helped the mason the way Peg had. Mistress Peg was able to heal the man's hand by asking questions and listening to the answers. By remembering what she had seen and heard, and what she had done before. For the first time Matilda wished not that Peg could hear Father Leufredus but that Father Leufredus could hear Peg.

Peg rubbed Stephen's thumb joint with ointment and herbs, then tightly wrapped it in the wet leather. "There. A most tidy job, if I do say so myself. Sit in the sun as much as you can today to hasten the leather drying. Come back to see me in seven days. And rest that well."

"Rest it? You mean not work?"

"Not with chisels. Not for a while. Maybe not ever, if you don't want to injure the hand again."

Stephen grew pale. "Not work? Mistress, what will become of us?"

"Go to Rufus Mason at the new Church of the Holy Blood. I tended his hand for him last year, and he is ever anxious to repay the favor. He will have work for you that does not involve chisels."

"What do I owe you, mistress?"

"Two pennies, which can wait until your hand is better and you have work."

"Thank you. And God bless you for your skill."

When Stephen had gone, Matilda turned to Peg. "He thinks you are a wonderworker like Master Theobald."

Peg shook her head, red curls springing from beneath her kerchief. "He might well think that, but I am not. I find my skills cannot help poor Grizzl. Her body grows daily more twisted and her cough harder, and Margery and I, who love her, can do nothing." She brushed the beginnings of tears from her eyes. "Even skill and love and care cannot overcome God's will."

"Then do you not waste your time?" asked Matilda.

Peg shook her head. "How can I know what God's will is? I just do what I can as well as I can."

And still Grizzl is dying, thought Matilda. *What good is all this effort?*

That night Matilda lay awake on her straw pallet, puzzling over God's will and Margery's skill and Grizzl's dying. Feeling confused and alone, she called on Saint Cyr for comfort, but the blessed saint said only,

Enough. I died before I was three. I know little of this world. Saint Elfleda responded that she was sent to an abbey as an infant so knew only praying and fasting and doing what she was told. That was no help. Matilda thought to call next on Saint Mary Magdalene, who certainly knew much about the world, but she was not at all sure that what that saint knew was what she wanted to know.

Tears prickled her eyes. When she finally fell asleep, she dreamed of people sick and suffering who begged her for help, but she had no hands and could only say over and over in Latin: *Volo, non valeo*—I would, but I cannot.

The next Sunday, when Matilda arrived back from Mass, she found Peg bustling about from Gilbert Carpenter to the red-haired brothers who sold salt and spices at the market to a tall man she did not recognize who lay silent as death on the table. The four had been carried to Peg's from the Shambles, where, drunk and fighting, they had slipped on bloody beef bones and knocked into each other, one after another, like ninepins.

Peg looked up from wrapping Gilbert Carpenter's wrist. "Matilda, thank Saint Modomnoc the Beekeeper, you are back! I need you to pound some comfrey, cut linen into strips, and—"

"It is Sunday, Mistress Peg, the Lord's day. Is it not a grievous sin to work on Sunday?"

Peg stopped wrapping and looked at the girl. "These men are injured and in pain. They've come to us for help. Would you turn away fellow human beings in pain because they are in pain on a Sunday?"

Matilda stood confused and unsure. Peg said, "Ah, have you learned nothing from me, for all your experience with pounding and pulling?" She finished wrapping Gilbert's wrist and started to bandage the elbow.

Matilda lay down on the floor with arms outstretched, so Peg had to step over her, and prayed for Peg's soul.

After a few minutes Matilda lifted her head to watch Peg. Her hands, chapped and red as they were, were as deft as a juggler's as she stepped to the unconscious man on the table and began to move his arms and legs, hands and feet about. Her smile, even though weary, cheered and eased her patients, doing as much to help them, Matilda saw, as her bandages, splints, and liniments. Matilda sighed, prayed to God for forgiveness in case she was wrong, and got up to help.

Peg smiled at her. "Good. This man's ankle is broken, and both wrists are sprained. We have to set and splint them all—and soon, before he wakes, for he is hard to handle even when he has not a belly full of ale. Now pound the comfrey."

Afterward Peg said, "Come and have a bite of supper. You have earned it. And my pleasure. And the gratitude of those men." With hands like tree roots, strong and sturdy, yet gentle as a pigeon's sound, she tore a piece of bread from a hard loaf. As Matilda chewed her own piece of bread, she watched Peg, feeling something like awe. Peg worked hard, earned little, ate poorly, was cold in the winter and would be hot in the summer. She saw friends suffer, patients die, and the unworthy prosper. Nevertheless she had more of laugh lines than frown lines marking the freckled surface of her face as she sat down happily to her bread-and-porridge supper, while Matilda sat tormented over having worked on Sunday, fearful that either Peg was wrong and Matilda had sinned, or Peg was right and Father Leufredus was wrong, and then where was Matilda?

She put her head in her hands. *Saint Perpetua,* Matilda prayed, *I am tormented and confused.*

My child, she heard the saint responding, *I was torn apart by wild beasts. I find it difficult to sympathize with your small worries.*

The trouble with saints, Matilda thought, was that you never could tell just what they would say.

CHAPTER ELEVEN

Easing Sarah

 On her way back from the market one day, smelling strongly of the fish heads and onions she carried, Matilda stopped by to greet Tildy, as had become her habit. "Fat Annet just poured a bowl of frumenty over the cook," Tildy said. "I am afeared that her temper is growing worse as the days grow warmer. Best you not come here anymore, or we both may suffer the consequences." Tildy and Matilda agreed to meet instead at the town well each Wednesday and Friday when the bells rang for the hour of Sext, after dinner when the sun was highest in the sky.

Matilda thought herself fortunate all the way home. Peg was so much kinder than Tildy's Fat Annet and never begrudged her helper time for a visit or a gossip or a getting-lost walk around the town.

When she entered the shop, she was surprised—knowing Peg was out seeing to Matthew Carbuncle's broken hip—to hear someone move in the darkness. A rat? she thought. A cat? Or Father Leufredus come at last? Her heart jumped. She squinted to see through the dimness.

It was the rude boy from the street. "I am here to see Red Peg the Bonesetter," he said. He peered closely at her. "You? The small girl with the green eyes and dimpled chin? Surely a miracle has brought us together again."

"Muddy Walter, I see," the girl said, dizzy with disappointment. "Peg is my mistress. She is not here, but you can tell me what is it you want of her."

"My master is Nathaniel Cross, the apothecary. His wife, Sarah, who suffers many ailments, is now much afflicted with pains in her legs. Nathaniel thought Peg might have some lotion or tonic to soothe them."

"I will ask Peg when she returns."

"It would help greatly if you were to bring it, for I am most fearsomely busy." Walter moved toward the door. "We must move from our large shop in the High Street. We will be the new tenants of Mother Uffa's small, dark shop. Your neighbors." At that the boy smiled.

Matilda pitied Nathaniel's predicament and would

not mind having him for a neighbor. She was less sure about this boy, who both irritated and intrigued her. She shrugged. "Mayhap I could bring the tonic tomorrow."

"And what is the name of the valued bonesetter's helper we will be indebted to?" Walter asked.

"Matilda."

"Well, Matilda the Bonesetter, we are grateful. No, that is much too big a name for someone as small as you. Let me rather say, Matilda Bone, we are grateful."

"As well you should be, Walter Mudd."

He left her.

Matilda Bone, she thought. Never had she been called any name but Matilda. Or clerk's daughter. Or priest's girl. *Matilda Bone*. It sounded well enough, although she would have preferred Saint Matilda or Matilda the Wise.

The next day there was a commotion at the far, dark end of the alley as Nathaniel, Sarah, and Walter moved into Mother Uffa's old house. Peg rejoiced over her new neighbors and the bouts of draughts that promised. She mixed a lotion of monkshood, meadowsweet, and oil of wintergreen, and rubbed it into Matilda's legs to demonstrate the proper application. "I would see to Sarah myself," she said to Matilda as she smoothed and rubbed, "but Sarah and I would get lost in chatter and she would never rest. She must rest.

There," she said to Matilda with a soft slap. And Matilda set off for Nathaniel's, her legs still stinging from the wintergreen and burning from the rubbing.

The shutters were closed when Matilda approached the shop, so she knocked softly. "Come in, whoever you be," she heard from within. Opening the door a crack, she peeked in. It looked like a wizard's work-room. The air was smoky and heavy with the sweet smells of herbs, spices, and magic, and the room was so dark that bits of daylight shone like tiny stars through the chinks in the wall. As her eyes grew accustomed to the darkness, Matilda could see shelves of bottles and jars, beakers and flagons covering the walls. Leaves, barks, branches, and herbs sprouted from the ceiling. In the center of the room was a long table on which bowls of mustard-yellow clay, wooden pestles, weights, and scales were piled.

"Come in, come in, girl, and shut the door, lest ye let in the cold, the tax collector, and all the creatures that prowl the streets," said a voice as crackled and whispery as dry leaves. Matilda stepped slowly inside and closed the door behind her.

"Closer, so I can see you." Matilda walked slowly toward the voice, which seemed to be coming from a bundle of clothes near the table. Upon closer inspec-tion the bundle proved itself a tiny round woman, with a face as wrinkled and soft as an old glove left outside in the rain. She was seated in a chair like a throne, with a carved back and lions' paws to rest her arms on—a chair such as a queen might have. At her feet lay two sleeping cats. Several more sprawled over the table. And on the woman's lap, one leg raised in the air and held there as she ceased her licking to examine the girl, sat Hag.

"You must be the Matilda Nathaniel told me was coming," the woman said. "I said to him, 'Nathaniel,' I said, for I only call him Master Cross when I am angry with—"

"Enough, Sarah, my dumpling," said Nathaniel, coming in with his arms full of bundles and baskets. "Now, who is this come to see us?"

"It is I, Matilda."

"Matilda? Matilda? Do I know a Matilda?" he asked.

"Matilda, from Peg's."

"Matilda who? And Peg who?"

Matilda was confused. It was only yesterday he had sent Walter. Could he have forgotten? Were his wits addled as well as his eyes? "I am from Red Peg the Bonesetter, come with a lotion for Sarah's legs. Walter calls me Matilda Bone."

"Oh, Matilda *Bone*. Why didn't you say so? Welcome, welcome," said the apothecary.

"Nathaniel, you old buffoon, do not vex the girl," said Sarah. "Why, I remember once when you—"

"Cease, my dear. You know you would talk until Judgment Day if you could, but Matilda has come to bring a soothing tonic for your legs, not to listen to an old woman's gossip."

Nathaniel smiled sadly at the girl. "Sarah," he said softly, "makes up with her tongue for the weakness of her legs, although talking makes her tired and her breath grows labored." He glanced at the seated woman with love and worry in his face. "I fear being helpless and unable to work, but if God must take something from me, better my sight than my wife."

Walter entered then, hidden behind the stack of rushes that he carried. At Nathaniel's word he dumped them onto the floor and lifted Sarah in his arms. "My lady, consider me your carriage. Where can I take you this day? The seashore? France or Italy? Or to London to see the King?"

"Just take me to my bed so Matilda can get about her work," Sarah said.

Matilda following, Walter carried Sarah into a small back room nearly filled with a straw mattress. Gently he put her on the bed. "Well, then, London will have to wait. Here, Matilda Bone. Ease our Sarah."

Matilda rubbed while Sarah dozed. "I will return

tomorrow," she said to Nathaniel after she finished. "Peg says I am to come after dinner each day, so I will come. Leastwise while I am still here. Until Father Leufredus comes back for me," she added softly.

So Matilda came each day with tonic for Sarah's legs. Each day as she arrived, Nathaniel asked, "Matilda who?" and Matilda answered, "Matilda Bone, from Red Peg. Do you not remember me?" long after she understood it was but a jest, for she did not know how else to respond.

Day after day as she rubbed the lotion into the legs of the sleeping Sarah, Matilda peered through the doorway, watching what went on. The cats busied themselves hunting the spiders, moths, mice, and other creatures that had invaded the shop. Walter came and went, waiting on customers, fetching armloads of thyme and parsley and mushrooms, and delivering filled bottles and jugs to those in need of them. Nathaniel was always there—pounding roots and leaves, weighing and bottling chopped mice, hanging bat wings to dry.

One day, as he prepared an ointment from goose grease and borage, she asked, "How can you tell one bottle from another if you cannot see their labels?"

"I have enough reading so I was once able to recognize the shapes of letters or identify the contents by their looks—their stems and leaves and flowers. But now as my eyes fail," Nathaniel said, sticking his long nose into bottles and bags, running his fingers through the leaves and stems, "I must tell them by their smell. Ah, here is sweet marjoram . . . bitterroot . . . tansy."

One day after Sarah fell asleep, Matilda spent a few minutes watching Nathaniel at work. The apothecary pulled a bottle off the shelf and gave it to Walter. "Here," he said, "take this woodruff to Master Stark at the grocers' guild." Walter took the bottle and, when Nathaniel turned around, exchanged it for another. Matilda gasped at his presumption and wondered whether to tell Nathaniel, but Walter grasped her arm and whispered, "I saw you watching me. Sometimes Nathaniel makes mistakes, picking up the monkshood instead of the comfrey root or the berries of the mistletoe instead of the juniper bush, but I watch him carefully and make things right. Nathaniel has taught me well."

"If you know so much, why do you stay here?" Matilda whispered back to him. "Surely you could do better with a proper apothecary who has a busier trade?"

"Being an apothecary requires more than merely reading labels. There is still much he knows that I do not."

This reminded Matilda of what Peg had said about

Tom, about different kinds of learning and knowing. She was no longer so sure it was not true.

"And I am fond of him," Walter continued. "I would never abandon him, no matter how much more 'proper' another apothecary might be." In spite of herself Matilda thought more kindly of Walter after this.

Frequently someone came to offer advice about Nathaniel's eyes. The daughter-in-law of Old Agnes the witch said she could do wonders with chicken blood and nail clippings. Peter Threadneedle suggested Nathaniel wash his eyes with onion juice and spit on a toad at midnight. Old Olaf applied a hemlock salve he had brought from the north and watched all night to make sure he had not used too much hemlock, thus killing Nathaniel instead of curing him. Still Nathaniel's sight grew no better.

With her prayers each night Matilda requested God's assistance for Nathaniel's eyes. She felt sorry for the kindly old man, and she liked the sound of "When but fourteen years of age, the holy Matilda effected the cure of a blind apothecary." *Dear Lord*, she prayed, *just as You miraculously provided leather so that Saints Crispin and Crispinian could make shoes for the poor, please provide a miracle so that Master Nathaniel may see well again. And while you are about it, could You please think about helping Sarah?*

And O *Saint Leger, who suffered the removal of your saintly eyes and tongue, please ask God to help Nathaniel. Saint Lucy, you who plucked out your own eyes and had them miraculously restored, please help Nathaniel's sight. Good Saint Clarus, whose name means* clear, *please help one whose vision isn't.* Clear. Thank you.

Amen, said the saints, for once neglecting to talk back to her.

A week of this had gone by when Sarah said, "My Nathaniel, an old donkey has an old eye. You must accept it. Well, we know it happens to many, and it has become clear that there is nothing to be done for it."

Matilda wondered if perhaps she had not been praying properly. Surely if she was doing it right, God would heed her. But God did not.

Consulting Master Theobald

 After Easter Day the earth began to warm and grow again. The winds blew soft and sweet. Peddlers offered rosemary and bay, fresh green parsley, and young white radishes.

For many days Matilda had been thinking about Nathaniel. Prayer was not helping him. Was God not listening?

The talk in the market was all of Master Theobald, who had cured Martha Threadneedle of excessive melancholy by a compound of viper's flesh and other ingredients known only to him. Maybe here was a cure for Nathaniel.

"Have you consulted the master physician, Theobald?" she asked Nathaniel. "He is famous and learned. Perhaps he knows of something more to do."

Sarah said, "The master physician does not bother with the likes of us."

"I would not know how to approach him," added Nathaniel. "Nor would we have coins enough."

Nathaniel's and Sarah's faces took on a look of overwhelming sadness that touched Matilda to the heart. "I know someone who lives in his house. Mayhap she can help."

At dinner Matilda said, "Can you do without me for a time tomorrow, Mistress Peg? I am thinking of going to Master Theobald to seek help for Nathaniel's eye troubles."

Peg shook her head and said, "I am not at all certain that anyone can help Nathaniel, but I would not tell you not to try."

So on a damp, green morning Matilda went again to the master physician's house. This time she walked right up to the house—gabled and garlanded, timbered and tiled—and found herself facing a thick oak door studded with iron, banded with brass, and fitted with a huge, heavy door knocker in the shape of a fiend from Hell with a man struggling in his mouth. It was the knocker that discouraged Matilda. How could she ask something of a man who had such a knocker? She hoped Tildy would have an idea.

Going round by the kitchen, Matilda found Tildy

alone, scrubbing down the big cook table with river sand. "I am sorry to come here after your warning, but I need to talk with you."

"It is all right," said Tildy, stopping for a moment. "Fat Annet is at her sister's for a wedding."

Matilda told her about Nathaniel and his eyes. "Do you think Master Theobald might be able to help? Will he see me?"

Tildy thought for a moment, chewing on a fingernail. Finally she said, "I believe I can persuade him."

Tildy dished up Master Theobald's dinner of stewed hare. Her bare feet whispered on the stone floors as she carried it down the hall, Matilda following. "Wait here," Tildy said as she entered Master Theobald's study.

"Master Theobald," Matilda heard her say, "there is a person here to see you. She seeks a cure for her employer's eye troubles. He has talked to everyone in town, but no one has been able to help. Now they think Master Theobald is the only man who could solve this problem. Theobald the Wonderworker you are called, great sir. That is why she is here."

Matilda could not hear the words of Theobald's rumbling response from where she stood, but she knew the way of it when Tildy came back. "He will see you," she whispered.

Tildy showed Matilda into Theobald's study. Matilda looked about her in awe. The high-pitched roof was webbed with scarred, black beams, held up by carved creatures with hair of fire and great swollen tongues. The walls were covered by woven hangings where they weren't pierced by real windows, tall and narrow, the glass so thick and green that the outside looked as if it were underwater. Between the windows were shelves, with rows upon rows of clear flasks filled with liquids of lovely colors, from amber to pale pink. A red-cushioned chair carved with filigrees and curlicues was pulled up to a table where stood scales of gleaming gold, charts of the stars, and, wonder of wonders, books with green leather covers. Bright Turkey rugs covered the stone floor here and there. The room was considerably grander than Peg's shop and Nathaniel's, even grander than Lord Randall's hall, which did, after all, have but rushes on the floor.

With the sound of an impatient throat clearing, Master Theobald made his presence known.

"I am here, great Master Theobald," Matilda said in a small voice, "but it is not I who am ailing. It is the apothecary Nathaniel Cross. Shall I go and fetch him?"

"Any physician who cannot diagnose at a distance is not worth the name of wonderworker," said Master

Theobald, taking the little book from his belt and licking a finger to turn the page. "Tell me where and when exactly was this Nathaniel of yours born?"

"I do not know, but I can discover it," Matilda said.

She ran back through the drizzle to Nathaniel's shop to ask the day and place of his birth and back again to Theobald's, where she dripped water on his stone floors as she repeated the information.

Theobald checked this chart and that chart, made some calculations, and licked his finger again. "Since the man was born under the sign of Gemini with Capricorn descending, it is no wonder the trouble is in his eyes." Theobald licked another finger. "At what time of year did the trouble start?"

"I must go again to Nathaniel," said Matilda.

"Hmm, a time of malign conjunction of Saturn and Mars," Theobald muttered on Matilda's return, licking more fingers and turning more pages. "What dreams has he had lately, especially those about toothaches or floods?"

Matilda confessed she did not know. "How can I succeed in curing him if you run away every time I ask a question?" Theobald grumbled.

When a breathless Matilda returned with what information she could get, Theobald handed her a basket that cradled a wondrous clear glass flask. "I need a sample of his urine, passed before the sun reaches the meridian."

Matilda complained silently as she took the basket and trudged again to Nathaniel's shop. Nathaniel once again gave Matilda what she asked, and the girl ran back to Theobald's.

"I cannot continue if you persist in running in and out," Theobald said.

"Great master," Matilda interrupted, wringing her damp kirtle out, "if you could please tell me everything you need from Nathaniel at one time, I would not have to run . . ."

Theobald glowered at her.

"I beg your pardon for interrupting," she said softly.

Master Theobald held the flask of urine to the candlelight. "Hmm," he said, and "Hmm" and "Hmm."

"What?" asked Matilda. "Hmm what?"

Theobald slapped the flask down on the table so hard that the liquid in the glass container splashed and sloshed like a small storm on a tiny sea. "According to Gilles de Corbeil's *De Urinis*, there are twenty-nine observations I must make of this: Is it ruddy or pale? milky, clear, or dark? thick or thin? frothy or flat? does it taste sweet or salty? and so on—and I cannot do it with a gnat buzzing in my ear."

Matilda sat down and pressed her lips together

tightly. Theobald held up the flask again, tilted it this way and that, smelled it, and then held it next to several of the flasks lining the walls of the room. Matilda was startled. All those lovely, sparkling, jewellike liquids were urine? Who would have thought it so beautiful?

"Hmm," Theobald said again, and consulted his book. "Did this vision problem come on suddenly?"

"No," said Matilda. "Nathaniel says it has long been coming on but now is worse than ever."

"Ah, then it is most likely not noxious gas in the stomach. Has he recently had a fever of any sort?"

"No, but for his eyes, he seems marvelously well. Except that he is sad and troubled. And discouraged."

"Good. It is not then a brain abscess brought on by overly hot bodily humors. Is he plagued by mental oversensitivity?"

Matilda was not exactly certain what that meant but told Master Theobald she was certain Master Nathaniel was plagued by nothing but poor eyesight.

"Ah, then since I have eliminated the other possibilities, the problem must be one of the visual spirit. When a man grows old, he tends to develop moisture in the visual spirit as it pours out of the brain, and his sight fails. Your apothecary must do this: Avoid all oil and moisture-making foods. No beans, no fish, no milk. I don't suppose he could afford crushed pearls in wine or the boiled rags of an Egyptian mummy?"

At Matilda's murmured "No," he continued, "Then he must, twice a day, inhale dried marjoram and purify his system with purgative pills and my special bitter mixture." Master Theobald swept up a pen and a sheet of parchment and wrote in a flowing hand.

He held the sheet above Matilda's reach and said, "This will without fail restore his sight. My fee is sixty pence."

Matilda was shocked. "Sixty pence? I do not know if Master Nathaniel has that much. Why, I doubt he earns sixty pence in a month."

"Then he needs to charge more. *De nihilo nihil*— nothing comes from nothing. Sixty pence."

Matilda shook her head.

"It is no wonder all the great physicians have required payment before treatment," Theobald said, pointing to his door. "Go."

Matilda left the room. He had written the prescription in Latin, not troubling to hide the page, never thinking the bonesetter's little maid could read what was written there: *One part pounded earthworm, one part ants' eggs, two parts bull urine, the fat of a medium-sized viper, and a pinch of asses' dung.*

Matilda found Tildy again in the kitchen and told

her what had transpired. "I know the remedy, Tildy! It was written in Latin and I could read it. It appears my Latin will help cure someone after all! Master Nathaniel will have his first dose before nightfall."

Tildy looked sharply at Matilda. "Do you not think that is cheating Master Theobald?"

Matilda felt a pang of guilt. It *was* cheating. Was it also a sin? Would she have to do penance? Mayhap. But later. First she would cure Nathaniel.

Peg, when Matilda told her what happened, said, "By the bones of Saint Polycarp, seems your reading is good for something."

Sarah was impressed that the mighty physician had sent a remedy for her Nathaniel. Nathaniel had enough faith in the physician to try the mixture. Everything but the asses' dung was available in the shop. A grumbling Walter took a shovel and soon supplied what was lacking, with enough left over for ten or twelve years of treatments.

While Matilda boiled the brew, a rag tied across her nose to mask the smell, Walter carried Sarah away from the stink. Nathaniel held his nose and drank the potion. He gagged and shouted, drooled and spat. But he kept it down.

After three days of doses, his eyes were no better. Herb and spice sellers would not enter the reeking shop, customers bypassed the entire alley, and Sarah refused to kiss Nathaniel good night. Nathaniel threw the remaining ants' eggs and asses' dung into the alley, whereupon he was cited by the Beadle of the Ward for contributing to the foulness of the city and had to pay a sixpence fine.

Matilda wanted to try again. She did not doubt Master Theobald's remedy. Perhaps she had remembered the recipe wrong or mixed it badly.

"No more," said Nathaniel. "I will try no more."

"There is nothing more to try," said Sarah.

Matilda continued her chores in silence, praying as she worked, trying to pierce the heavens with her prayers and reach the heart of God. God, she knew, must have good reason for not helping Nathaniel, but she was fond of him and he was a good man and she could not just leave him and Sarah to suffer and to starve. There must be something more she could do, but what? Matilda worried until her head hurt, but Saint Denis, when called upon for aid, said only, *Your head aches? I had no head*, and Nathaniel dosed her with a tincture of dropwort and birch.

CHAPTER THIRTEEN

Talking to Effie

Early one morning as Matilda was emptying the chamber pot into the gutter outside, she heard an uproar. Tucking the pot under her arm, she followed the noise around the corner, where Blood and Bone Alley met Frog Road. A crowd had gathered around a blond-bearded giant in a plaid kilt who was grabbing at folk and shouting, "Is there no' a doctor in this wee town? Is there no one to help?" as his horses milled about him, packs askew and spilling onto the road.

The enormous scissors advertising Tomas Tailor's shop hung from one chain, dented and bent. On the ground lay a woman, a gash on her forehead and a look of pain on her face. The giant shouted again, "Is there no one to help?"

Of the wrong kind of help there was plenty. Beggars

helped themselves to what fell from the packs, a wandering friar offered his prayers in exchange for pennies, merchants presented for sale linen cloth for bandages and wine for dulling pain, and Tomas shrieked about the bloody dent in his sign.

Someone shoved Matilda aside as he pushed his way through the crowd. It was Master Theobald. People whispered and stood back. "I am Theobald, master physician. What is amiss here?" he asked the bearded giant.

"My wife was shoved off the road by your English drunkards, knocked into the tailor's sign, and fell off her horse," the giant said. "She is sufferin' terrible. Ye can help us, can ye not?"

The injured woman moaned, and the giant grabbed Theobald's arm.

"Tell me," Theobald said, "the month and day she was born."

"I am lyin' here in the road like yesterday's barley bannock, my head achin' somethin' fierce, and you want to celebrate me birthday?" the woman said. "Enough."

"The help you require, woman, lies in *astris*, the stars. Therefore I need to know the month and day of your birth."

Matilda watched Master Theobald closely. She did not understand why his mixture had failed to help

Nathaniel, but here was another chance for him to perform a miracle of healing, as he had so many times before.

"I be Hamish MacBroom," said the giant to Theobald. "This is my Effie, and she were born the day after Christmas near thirty year ago."

The physician consulted the book at his waist. "Move your arms this way," he said to Effie, "and that way. Try to sit. Now bend."

The woman obeyed, grunting and moaning as she did so. "I feel like the pig's dinner," she said. "Me side hurts like the Divil were dancin' on it."

Theobald turned to the giant, saying, "Take her up and come with me." Hamish MacBroom lifted Effie and carried her cradled like a babe in his big arms.

Matilda, still holding the chamber pot, followed along, eager to see Master Theobald's miracle. She assumed they were bound for the physician's great house, but instead the little procession turned into Blood and Bone Alley and entered Peg's shop, where Peg and Margery sat eating.

Sweeping remnants of bread to the floor, Peg had Hamish lay the woman down on the table. Theobald, bowing slightly to Margery and smiling an icy smile, said, "Mistress Lewes, and how do you find the ills of women this day?"

"Mostly the fault of men, Master Theobald," she said, bowing back to him. "Now, what have we here?"

Theobald ignored her and turned to Peg. "This woman has broken two or more of her ribs. Bandage them for her. I will send over a jar of my hare's-foot salve for the cut on her head." The physician left.

The giant looked at Peg and shouted, "*You* will tend my Effie?"

While he spluttered, Effie said, so softly all had to bend to hear, "Hamish MacBroom, you great sausage, stand out of the way and let her get on with fixin' me, for yif I die, I swear to come back and haunt you, you and the new young wife you will take."

The giant stepped back, and Peg said, "Take heart, little Effie. Why, I have mended more ribs than there are stars in the night sky." She wrapped a strip of linen around Effie's rib cage and pulled it tight. Effie moaned and fainted.

At that Hamish fainted also, but too big was he to be moved, so they left him where he fell and Peg worked around him.

Tildy came with Master Theobald's hare's-foot salve. "Smells like old meat," said Tildy, handing it to Matilda, "but the master has healed many with it."

"This Effie is fortunate such a man as Master Theobald is caring for her," said Matilda with a glance at Margery, "else she would surely die." Doctor Margery took the salve from Matilda, smelled it, and spread it gently on Effie's forehead. Tildy nodded and left.

Hamish awoke and was doctored next with warm ale seasoned with pepper. "She will live," Peg said to him, "but she should not be moved for a sevennight. Let her stay here, where I can watch her."

Hamish carried Effie to Matilda's bed in the buttery, where she could have a bit of rest.

All was quiet in the shop that day, for no one wished to disturb Effie. That night Matilda slept in Peg's bed, her sleep soft and deep in that warm place that smelled of Peg and sausages.

Effie stayed in Matilda's bed for seven days and nights, but Peg got her own bed back, and Matilda slept wrapped in a blanket on the floor. Peg kept an eye on Effie and checked her bandages now and then, muttering, "Hmm" and "Ohh." Master Theobald did not return or send to hear how she was doing. Instead, it was Margery who came unbidden each day and tended the woman. "How do you feel?" she asked. And "Does this hurt?" and "Can you move this way?" Matilda feared Margery would undo all of Theobald's good work, but Effie did not send her away.

"You, Matilda, you do this, too, each day," Margery said, pressing her ear to Effie's chest to hear her heart and her lungs. "If you hear a soft crackling sound, it means her lungs have been pierced and we must despair of her. Thus far I hear nothing amiss, but we must keep listening." Matilda was about to say that she was Peg's helper and not Margery's, but Peg huffed and narrowed her eyes, so Matilda said nothing and just nodded.

When Effie's head wound showed signs of putrefaction, Doctor Margery cleaned it with warm wine, placed cobwebs and a pinch of bread mold gently over it, and bound it all together with clean linen. Although Matilda looked and looked, she never did see Master Theobald's salve again.

Matilda worried that if Effie did heal, Margery would take the credit for it. But once Margery was sure that Effie was mending, she left most of the tending to Matilda, who listened to her chest, changed her bandage, brought warm ale for her stomach and cold cloths for her head, and asked her how she did and was all well with her.

One night after Peg was asleep and Hamish back in his bed at the inn, Effie leaned over and shook Matilda's shoulder. Matilda, fearing that Effie had been taken worse, jumped up. "I will get Peg," she said.

"No. Dinna bother Peg." By the dim light from the fire in the other room, Matilda could see Effie shake her bandaged head. "It's just that I am near daft from this achin'. Peg gave me a wee dram of poppy juice, but still my side aches some'ut fierce. Perhaps if you talked to me, I could forget it. I know you are wretched tired from working all day, little Matilda, but I sorely need your company."

Matilda was taken aback. *What can I say to this bandaged stranger?* She thought for a moment. *If I ask Effie questions*, she realized, *she must do the talking. That may serve just as well.*

So Matilda searched her mind for a question and asked Effie, "Do you think spring is finally here?"

"Not inside this cold, dark shop," answered Effie.

And another: "Did you know an eel with a big head is no bargain?"

Effie answered, "I think any eel is no bargain."

And one to which Matilda truly wanted to know the answer: "How long does it take a priest to ride to London and back?"

"Depends on the priest," Effie said.

There was silence. Matilda thought she was not doing well at getting Effie to talk. Perhaps Matilda's questions were at fault. She thought a minute and then asked Effie, "How did you come to be here with Hamish? I can hear that you are not local born."

"I come from the Border Country along the wall

that Hadrian built so long ago," Effie said, "where the heather grows purple in the sun and the grass ripens into gold. With six daughters before me, my parents promised me, the youngest, to the Convent of Saint Finbar if the next child be a boy."

"And was it?" Matilda asked as Effie paused. This was better. Effie, like Peg and Father Leufredus, was happier talking about herself to an interested listener.

"Aye, it was—Finbar, a right sturdy boy with my father's red hair and red nose. But my mother died in the havin' of him. They sent me to the sisters as promised, but the nunnery was not for me, all prayers and poor food and thinkin' on God instead of people. When Hamish came one night and stole me, I was not at all unwilling, me thinkin' God had truly cheated on His part of the bargain, takin' my mother like He did. Besides, in those days Hamish was the most beautiful man in the dale."

"But you broke your promise to God."

"Not mine, little Matilda. And is it not true, as Saint Paul says, that all sacrifices are as nothing in comparison with love, which purifies and brightens the heart?"

There was silence as Matilda struggled with Effie's words. Love brightens and purifies the heart? Never had she heard such a thing from Father Leufredus. She was beginning to think there was much she had never heard from Father Leufredus that she would like to hear now.

Into the silence Effie moaned, hand to her head, pale face grown paler still. Matilda, fearful of Effie's pain and anxious to relieve it, found her tongue and began to talk. "I myself was raised on Lord Randall's manor a day's ride from here, with servants and Father Leufredus for tutor. We wore dresses of crimson samite and Spanish leather boots and ate cheese from our own cows fragrant with the rich green grass the cows fed on. Never did I have to sweep or eat sausage, for I was used to better things."

"How then did you come to this poor place?" Effie asked. She had stopped moaning. Matilda could see that her talking was helping, so she hurried on.

"Father Leufredus brought me. I am here only to await his return. Or a summons to join him in London."

"Yet I am glad you are here now, to tend me and listen to me of a long night. To help me live." Effie reached out and patted Matilda's hand.

"It was fortunate for you Master Theobald was there to see to you," Matilda said.

Effie snorted. "The man talked like a fool, would not listen to anyone, and did not even look at me."

"But he is a great wonderworker. Everyone says so. And he did save your life."

"No. It were you and Peg and the bigfooted Doctor Margery."

"In that case it was *truly* a miracle you survived."

"No, I think the miracle was the skill of Margery and Peg and your kind heart. And the will of God." She crossed herself.

Matilda could see in her mind Effie, bright with health, riding her horse through purple heather and golden grass. As much as she wished to argue with her about the merits of Master Theobald and the faults of Doctor Margery, Matilda said only, "Amen."

There was silence again until Effie said, "Tell me more of Matilda."

Matilda was ready to speak further of bright dresses and warm fires but stopped. She found herself wanting to tell Effie things she had rarely thought about and certainly had never told anyone. Maybe because she was hidden there in the darkness. Matilda did not know. She sighed and began again, slowly. "My mother was a brewer's daughter who married Lord Randall's clerk, gave birth to me, and, tiring of marriage and motherhood, left us both soon after."

"No! Did she nivver come back?"

"Never. My father and I lived at Lord Randall's

manor, where my father taught me Latin and reading and writing and then, when I was six, died at his desk. Of too much drink, I was told. Lord Randall did what he considered his Christian duty. I was given to be fed by the manor servants and tutored by the manor priest."

"And so ye lived well in a great house, eating fine food and wanting for nothing."

"Yes, I . . ." Matilda stopped and shook her head. *No. I wanted for much,* she thought. And once thought, it had to be said. "No. I wanted for much. The house was great, but no part of it was mine; the food fine, but given begrudgingly. I lived somewhere between servants and those they served." She shook her head again. She had been lonely there. Why had she not known that?

"And the priest?" Effie asked her.

"Father Leufredus found me willing and clever, so he raised me to be saintly, meek, and obedient, above the things of this world. When he left the manor, he brought me to Peg. I had nowhere else to go. But he has not come back or sent for me."

"And what will ye do now?"

Matilda was silent for a moment before replying, "I do not know. I cannot stay in this place. I know so little of what matters here. I cannot heal the sick like

Master Theobald or mend bodies like Peg. I am use-less."

"Pish. I have been watchin' ye these days," said Effie. "Ye're far from useless. Ye must just use the tools God gave you. Why, a farmer could till a field with a horn spoon if he had to. Find your tools . . . and . . . put them . . . to good use." There was silence. Effie had drifted off to sleep.

While Effie slept, Matilda's thoughts ran around and around in her head. She thought about living at the manor, being lonely, using her own tools. Why had she spoken so freely to Effie? Was she right to do so? All the same, she had a sweet, full feeling inside that warmed her, and soon she too slept, and all was silent in the little house with the bright-yellow bone on the door.

CHAPTER FOURTEEN

Sending a Letter

Often Matilda and Effie would talk quietly into the night, and Matilda grew fond of her. Too soon she and Hamish were leaving. Effie, her side still swaddled and head wrapped in linen to keep the wound clean, said farewell to Peg and Margery, who hugged and clucked and fussed. Then Effie turned to Matilda. "My prayers stay here with ye, Matilda," she said. "I wish ye well."

Matilda wanted to reply but instead gave Effie a little nod and turned her head to hide her tears.

Unable still to ride, Effie settled herself in a litter swung between two horses. She looked at Matilda once more and said quietly to Hamish, "I long to cuddle her like a babe, and sing to her as my mother sang to me: 'Hush thee, hush thee, dinna fret thee, the Divil willna get thee.' But she be too stiff and proud for cuddling." Matilda, overhearing, thought if Effie tried, she might not find Matilda as stiff and proud as she thought. But Effie did not try.

Matilda watched as the woman was carried away. Would she never be able to ride again? Would she always see the purple heather from behind the curtains of a litter? She lived, which did count for something, but would she never recover? Matilda shook her head. If only Master Theobald had tended Effie instead of Doctor Margery!

Matilda watched for a long while as the riders disappeared into the distance. Peg's little shop would seem very empty now.

Across the alley she saw Walter heading toward the apothecary shop. There was much she had neglected while tending Effie. She had failed to meet Tildy at the well. She had not seen to Sarah—Peg had done that. And she had not thought even once of Nathaniel's troubles. She would remedy this right now, she thought, as she wiped her hands on her skirt, patted her hair, and hurried off to Nathaniel's.

"Who is this here to see me? Do I know you?" asked Nathaniel as she entered.

She hesitated for a moment and then said loudly, "Who is this old man in Nathaniel's shop? Does he know you are here?"

Nathaniel smiled a big smile and nodded at her. "Welcome back, Matilda Bone. We have missed you."

"Has not Peg come to tend Sarah's legs?"

"Yes, but she is not you. People are not as replaceable as . . . as boots."

Matilda wondered for a moment if she should look behind her to see who Nathaniel was speaking to. But she knew it was she. He had missed her, and she smiled inside and out with pleasure.

"How is it you come here today, Matilda Bone?"

"Effie has gone, and I found myself wondering how your eyes do. I have not heard that your sight miraculously improved while I have been busy elsewhere, so I came to see for myself."

He shook his head. "No better, but I have Walter's help and my Sarah, so I try to be thankful for those. And what have you been busy elsewhere about?"

Matilda sat and told him about Effie and Hamish, and he listened and nodded. Finally she got up and said, "Forgive me. There is much I must attend to," and she was off.

Talking about Effie had reminded her of something Effie had said, and Matilda decided to try again to help Nathaniel, this time with her own tools. She had already tried her Latin and her prayers, and they had not worked. What else could she do but read and write? (And start fires, brew tonic, and bargain for fish, and she did not know how those could help Nathaniel.) Perhaps a letter? She could write a letter and ask someone very wise for help. Someone wise in medicine. But who?

Her father used to say the wisest minds in England were in Oxford. She would send a letter to Oxford.

Matilda hurried to the market, where she traded her pennies for parchment and ran back to Peg's. She smoothed the page, scraping off a bit of dirt here, a splash of something else there, taking time to smell the beloved, familiar smell. Carefully she took knife to quill to cut a sharp point, touched the tip to her tongue, dipped it carefully in the ink bottle, and wrote in Latin on the precious sheet, enchanted by the look of the words as they tumbled and trailed across the page:

Salutem dico *to the greatest of all physicians who reside at Oxford, whoever you may be, from Matilda of Blood and Bone Alley at the sign of the yellow bone, Chipping Bagthorpe:*

There is in this town an apothecary, by name Nathaniel Cross, who is patient and kind and full of loving but lately has been gloomy and disheartened, for his eyes have gone bad in such a way that he cannot see what is right in front of his face. He looks to starve or die if no one helps him. We have prayed, dosed, salved, and bled, to no end. Have you any knowledge of cures or miracles or remedies that might allow him to spend the days God has given him as an apothecary?

Please send word of any such to me, Matilda Bone, for I can read as well as write, although I fear it is not important like saving souls or saving lives and no one here seems to see the value of it at all.

I know Nathaniel's gratitude will be yours if you can assist him in this matter of seeing.

With all thanks and respect due your great physicianness, I am yours,
Matilda Bone

She spit on the tip of the quill and wiped it on her sleeve, cleaned the wooden ruler on her skirt, and capped the ink bottle. She carried her letter back to the market, where she found a tinker who was heading north to Oxford. He would for a price deliver her letter to the physicians' guild. "I have no silver," said Matilda.

"A kettle?" asked the tinker. "Good wooden spoons? A dress, well brushed and gently worn? Velvet slippers?"

"Naught but what I wear," said Matilda.

The tinker reached out and touched her shoulder. "This cloak looks old but of good English wool—I could get a few pennies for it."

Matilda hesitated. Spring was here and summer on the way. She could do without a cloak until fall, by which time who knew where she would be or whether she would need a cloak there. So off it came. The tinker took Matilda's letter, folded it, and tucked it carefully inside his shirt. "A few days only and your letter and I will reach Oxford." He rode away with her cloak and her letter, pots and pans and kettles clanking.

When Matilda returned, Peg was not at home. Nor was she there very often in the next few days. She was with Grizzl, who was failing despite Peg's care and Matilda's prayers. One day when primroses bloomed in the refuse in the alley, Peg and Margery came slowly in. "Grizzl has gone," Peg said to Matilda, her red and freckled face almost unrecognizable in its grief.

Matilda crossed herself. She pictured the little hobbled woman with the big smile. Poor gentle Grizzl was in Heaven now, but Matilda would miss her. Looking at Peg's pain, Matilda thought, *Grizzl should not have died!* And then she said it aloud. "Grizzl should not have died. Master Theobald should have been consulted. He would have known what to do."

"Enough, Matilda," said Peg as she put an arm about Margery's shoulder. "Enough." But still Matilda thought with sorrow, *I should have taken Master Theobald to Grizzl.*

There was no money for a coffin or a crier to call, "Pray God for the dead," but Matilda joined the small procession that carried Grizzl, wrapped in Peg's best bed linen, to the churchyard. Margery brought all her ends and pieces of candles to add to Peg's and Nathaniel's store, so each mourner had a bit of lighted candle to carry. Violets, buttercups, and columbine basked in the May sunshine and nodded their many-colored heads as the mourners passed by. The small bundle that had been Grizzl was laid in a grave near the apple tree. Matilda heard little of what the priest said because of the voice in her head that was saying she should have fetched Master Theobald, Master Theobald, Master Theobald.

Afterward the setting of bones went on. Alkelda Weaver brought the baby again and again. Peg pushed and pulled her legs; Matilda rubbed in an ointment of bittersweet and chamomile and gave her a decoction of wild strawberry and acanthus leaves to drink. After one visit Matilda offered to hold the child while her mother ate her dinner. The little girl smelled of strawberry and chamomile and warm baby sweat. She reached up and touched Matilda's face as softly as a fairy might. The touch sent warmth right down Matilda's body to her heart. She touched the baby's face in return and whispered, "Hush thee, hush thee, dinna fret thee, the Divil willna get thee."

CHAPTER FIFTEEN

Naming Birds

 The west wind blew warm. The May air was sweet with blossoms and sour with the smell of wet earth freshly turned over. The rumble of the dung carts carrying stable sweepings to spread on fields and garden plots sounded on the air like the moaning of lost souls.

Each day Matilda imagined where on the road her letter might be, who was reading it, what great physician was saying at that very moment, "Why, I have just the answer for this girl. Let me write and tell her."

One afternoon Matilda went again to the tanner's yard by the river, and Walter came along to help carry the bundles of hides. They sniffed deeply, reveling in the smell of new grass, baking bread, and drying mud.

On the way back they pulled off their boots and waded in the muck and puddles along the riverside, warmed by the sun. Boats and barges loaded with wood and wool and iron tools crowded the river.

"Aye, it's a grand day," said Walter.

Matilda said nothing but marveled at the beauty of the early summer, which she was accustomed to seeing only through the narrow window of the priest's study. Warmed by the air, she felt her body ease. A breeze blew sweetly like the breath of God, and the air was heavy with the song of birds.

"Never have I heard so many birds," said Matilda.

"They are not just birds," said Walter. "They have names. Those brown spotted birds calling *tchuck-tchick*, those are throstles. And the ones singing their song high in the sky are skylarks."

Matilda stopped still and watched the sky as Walter pointed at the birds. Of course they had names. Everything on God's earth had a name. "How do you know these things?" she asked him.

"I grew up in a village filled with birds like these. I also know about badgers and foxes, teasel and thistle, and many other things. I am at heart a countryman."

"Once," said Matilda softly, "you said my hair was as gold as the belly of an ouzel. What is an ouzel?"

"There," Walter pointed, "on that stone in the stream, that bird with the loud, bubbling song. That is a gold-bellied ouzel."

Matilda laughed. She laughed again as Walter imitated the *ha-ha-ha-ha-ha* of a woodpecker and the sad, sweet song of a willow warbler.

"Throstles, larks, the gold-bellied ouzel, woodpeckers, and willow warblers," said Matilda with pleasure. "I can say 'bird' in Latin and Greek but never knew their names. Now I can name them," and she did: *throstles and larks and gold-bellied ouzels, some woodpeckers and willow warblers.* "And I can sing them," and she did: *throstles and larks and gold-bellied ouzels, some woodpeckers and willow warblers.* Walter joined in and they danced a shy, clumsy dance there by the stream as they sang their summer song.

Soon they had to rest, so they sat side by side in the warm grass as the sky grew the mottled red and blue of the bruise on Matilda's leg left by the bite of one of Samson's geese. Matilda realized she now knew less about Walter than she knew about birds. "Tell me," she said, "how you came to Nathaniel."

"My mum sent me to be apprentice when I was eight," he said, and smiled. "When I first entered the large shop near the east market, my knees knocked together like cymbals. I thought surely I'd be sent home, puny and scared as I was. In my heart I yearned to go, but my empty belly knew that Mum had sent me for my own good."

Walter bent over double and screwed his face into a maze of laugh lines and wrinkles so that he looked more like Sarah than Sarah herself. "'Looks a mite small for doing what needs doing, Nathaniel,' Sarah said. 'I'm stronger than I look, sir,' I said to Nathaniel. 'I can wrestle Matthew down to the ground, and he has two years on me.'"

Matilda watched, fascinated, as Walter changed from Sarah back to Walter and then into a tiny bald-headed Nathaniel: "'Then I have no doubt of your strength. How are your brains?'

"'I know A from B and two plus two,' I answered him. 'That'll do. The rest you can learn,' said Nathaniel Cross. And so I stayed," Walter said, turning back into himself. He stretched and began to look about for his boots.

"Did you miss your home?" said Matilda, searching his face.

Walter shrugged. "I cried for Mum some, alone at night on my straw mat in that strange house in a strange town. Never before had I slept without Matthew and Martin snuggled up beside me, and the sound of Mum's snoring saying she was here and all was well. Still I stayed. I am here yet. And never now would I go from here." He looked at Matilda. "What of your mother? Do you miss her?"

Matilda thought for a moment, then said, "My mother ran off when I was a babe and—" She stopped suddenly, surprised to be confiding in Walter in the broad daylight, but then continued. "I was living there at the manor where my father was clerk, and when my father died, I became ward of Lord Randall . . . no, in truth, since I was there already, Lord Randall said, 'Let her stay but keep her out of my way,' and Father Leufredus said . . ." The words poured out of her like beans from a broken pot.

"Hold up. I cannot listen as fast as you talk," said Walter.

Matilda looked down at her feet and then up into Walter's impudent, friendly, familiar face. "These boots," she whispered, pulling them back on, "are all I have that is truly mine. They belonged to my father. All else was given me by those at the manor and taken back when I was sent away. I am more welcome in Peg's little shop than ever I was in that fine house." She looked at Walter. "Never have I told anyone this. I myself did not know it."

There was silence for a moment as they loaded Walter's back with hides and continued on their way. "Last night I had a dream about Hell," Matilda said as they walked. "Beelzebub was dining on roast heretic with garlic sauce. I was there, but was I dinner guest or dinner I do not know."

"You think much on demons," said Walter.

"Father Leufredus taught me well to fear them and the roiling sea of fire that is Hell."

"What about God's love?"

God's love. Walter must know a different God than she did, remembering Father Leufredus's warnings about Hellfire and punishment and God's anger. Now she thought of it, so did Tildy, who spoke of laughing prayers. "Father Leufredus was not one to speak much of love," she said at last.

"I do not doubt that," said Walter.

"I used to think it would please God if I became a martyr," Matilda went on, "but when faced with the choice of death by fire, drowning, or disemboweling, I decided it was sufficient to have learning and Latin. Now it happens that is worth nothing at all here."

Walter looked puzzled. "You're a strange duck, Matilda."

"In truth I feel much like a duck, a duck living among chickens. I walk differently, cluck differently. I used to think it was the chickens who were strange, but now I do not know."

"My mum used to say, 'Ducks may be useless birds, but only a duck can lay a duck egg.'"

Matilda looked at him sharply. Did he mean that she, too, was useless? But what she saw in his face made her think she was being comforted, so she smiled, and they walked in silence all the way back to Peg's.

CHAPTER SIXTEEN

Tending Tildy

May warmed and deepened, promising to turn into summer soon. More customers came with assorted breaks, sprains, strains, and attendant ill tempers. Tom came back, and the small shop was again filled with the sounds of whispering and laughter. Matilda felt alone and restless. She had just told Walter that she felt welcome at Peg's shop, and now she felt welcome nowhere. Her mind was all *ab hoc et ab hac*, here and there, and so were her feet.

"Go," said Peg. "Somewhere else. I can pace and sigh as well myself," said Peg. "And, Matilda, there is no need to hasten back."

It being Friday and nearly the hour of Sext, Matilda headed for the well in the market square. She would see Tildy, and Tildy would make her laugh.

Matilda sat down next to Tildy on the well's edge.

Before either girl could open her mouth, Fat Annet rushed up, waving a basket cradling a joint of beef. "There you are, you lazy nincompoop!" she shouted. "Lollygagging and leaving *me* to face the butcher." She struck Tildy sharply with the basket and stomped off. Tildy teetered for a moment and then fell right into the well, banging her head sharply on the edge. The well was shallow enough for Matilda to reach Tildy's feet but deep enough for her head to be in the water.

Lucy Goode the rosary maker and Tomas Tailor's skinny wife, wet from laundry, tucked up their skirts and helped Matilda pull Tildy out. She was breathing, but shallowly, face pale, big cut on her forehead streaming blood, tinting the water the color of sunset. Matilda feared for her. Would she die, as Grizzl had?

Lucy shook her head. "So much blood."

"That Annet ever was hotheaded and brutish," said the tailor's wife. "The girl will likely die."

"*Saliva mucusque!* She will not die! I will fetch someone to help," Matilda said. She ripped a strip of cloth from her kirtle (not without regret, for it was her only kirtle) and wrapped it around Tildy's head. "I will return as soon as I can," she said. "Don't let her die!"

Matilda ran as fast as she was able, her bare feet tripping over cobblestones and splashing through the slimy water that ran down the middle of the streets, thinking, *Tildy cannot die*. Matilda could not wrap her in linen and put her in the ground, as Grizzl had been put. *Tildy cannot die! I must find Master Theobald*, she thought. *Please God he is at home*.

Matilda ran through the market square, skirt flapping about her ankles and hair tangled about her face. At the turning to Master Theobald's, she found herself slowing down, strangely reluctant to go farther. *I must fetch Master Theobald*, she told herself. *He is the town's leading physician*.

He talked like a fool, said Effie's voice. *And he failed to help Nathaniel*, Matilda's own voice added in her mind.

"*Saliva mucusque!* What shall I do?" She turned in the direction of Blood and Bone Alley and ran to ask Peg's advice. But Peg was not there. Nor were Nathaniel and Walter. They were gathering wood sorrel and birthwort root, Sarah said, and would not be home until supper.

Another *Saliva mucusque!* as Matilda sat down to catch her breath. What would Father Leufredus suggest? Probably he would pray and quote Saint Augustine. That was no help. She thought a moment. Whom could she trust? Who would help her? And the answer that came surprised her. *Doctor Margery*.

No, she thought, jumping up. *Not Doctor Margery, with her big feet and wrong-headed opinions*.

But yes, her mind said again. *Doctor Margery with her clever fingers and common sense.*

Master Theobald saved Effie.

No, that was Peg and Doctor Margery.

She let Grizzl die.

No, her mind said. *Grizzl died despite Margery's attention, not because of it.*

Mistress Margery, came Peg's voice, *whatever you may think, is twice the physician, three times the person, and at least four times a better soul than that person who calls himself Master Theobald.*

But Margery had no learning, no languages. How would Matilda ever explain it to Father Leufredus?

Finally she bit her lip and said aloud, "I need not explain it to Father Leufredus. I must do what I think best." She ran back toward Frog Road, where she knew Margery lived.

"Doctor Margery? Doctor Margery?" she asked passersby until one of them pointed out a tiny cottage between a barber-surgeon's shop and the Prince and Hedgehog Tavern.

Matilda arrived at Margery's door and pulled it open, as disheveled and red of face as the woman herself.

"Peg? Is aught amiss with Peg that you should come to my house?" Margery asked.

"No, it is not Peg but Tildy. My friend Tildy."

Matilda paused a moment, panting for breath, and then hurried on. "I sorely need your help. Tildy was pushed into the well. She is battered and bleeding and will not wake. Please go and look at her."

"Well, then, let us hurry and see what can be done for the poor mite," said Doctor Margery, putting things into a bag.

As Doctor Margery hastened to Tildy, Matilda went looking for Tom and his wagon. She knew where Saint Brendan was stabled, and there was Tom, sharing turnips and onions with the ox. He yoked Saint Brendan, and they raced back to the market square. In truth they did not race. Matilda's thoughts raced. Her heart raced. But Saint Brendan ambled as he always did, despite Tom's pulling and shouting in Latin.

A crowd of people was gathered about when they arrived, but all were strangely quiet. Doctor Margery was kneeling beside Tildy, who lay still on the ground. "No!" Matilda cried as she jumped from the wagon and ran to Tildy. "No!"

Doctor Margery looked up at Matilda. "Hush, she still lives," the doctor said. Matilda crossed herself in relief as Tom gathered Tildy in his arms. He deposited her gently in the wagon and drove to Doctor Margery's, where he placed her carefully in the doctor's bed before taking himself and Saint Brendan away.

Margery washed Tildy's face. She felt her head and limbs, looked into her eyes and mouth and ears, listened to her chest, and thumped her here and there, while Matilda hovered like a mother bird.

Finally the doctor said, "She has no broken bones, but I think her skull has been fractured, in which case bits of bone endanger her. Her head must be opened further and any pieces removed." She took her knife to Tildy's head and began to clean the wound.

"Are you not afraid the Devil will enter her head through that great hole?" Matilda asked, suddenly worried. Had she done right to fetch Margery?

"It may well be," said Margery. "But there is nothing I can do to prevent that. It is more likely that dirt and sharp bits of bone will enter, and that at least is preventable by careful cutting and cleaning. In any case, a doctor who is afraid is good for nothing. All is in God's hands."

Matilda watched, astonished, as Margery cleaned the wound with a solution of water betony and sanicle, then put her fingers inside Tildy's head. Matilda's innards groaned and leapt, as if she were spinning herself dizzy, at the sight of so much blood.

The doctor's face glowed red, shiny with sweat, but her hands remained steady and sure as she anointed the wound with bread mold and a salve of mandragora fruit and sewed it closed just as a tailor might. She covered the wound with cobwebs, wrapped a bandage tightly about Tildy's head, and then looked up. Her smile was gentle, and her blue eyes brimmed with compassion. "I have hope she will live, but she may have lost too much blood, or the wound may turn putrid." She lifted the still-sleeping Tildy up and gently poured some foul-smelling tonic down her throat. "She will sleep quite a while now. We can but watch and wait."

Doctor Margery went out, but Matilda sat by her bed all day, watching over Tildy. Had she done right to call Margery? Matilda wondered again. She looked around her as if she could find some clue there.

The doctor had only one small room, but that was, to Matilda's surprise, neat and clean. Knives and other instruments were kept in a small chest, there were bottles and jugs on a table, and herbs hung from the ceiling over the fire pit. There were no books and no astrological charts. Matilda sighed. She had done what she thought best for Tildy, and she was determined to help Margery to help Tildy in any way she could.

That evening Margery returned with a meat pie for Matilda. "I have gone to Peg," Margery said, "to ask if you might stay here for some days. I cannot tend your Tildy and deliver babies at the same time. I need your help. Will you stay?" Matilda nodded, pleased to be needed and happy to stay near Tildy.

Each night, wrapped in Doctor Margery's cloak, she slept on the floor near the sleeping Tildy while Doctor Margery curled at the end of the bed. Each morning and evening the doctor gave Tildy the foul-smelling syrup. Every few hours she would return from this house or that cottage to check on her and give Matilda instructions. The rest of the day Matilda cared for Tildy. When Tildy grew restless and feverish, she wrapped her in cool, wet linen, praying as she did so. She tucked quilts around Tildy's thin body when the chills began. She cleaned Tildy's head wound with wine and changed the bandage. At times Tildy's breathing grew so slow and labored that Matilda thought to run for a priest, but she did not wish to leave her friend alone.

One morning Matilda woke to find Tildy's lips blue and her face pale as death. Doctor Margery was sitting beside the bed, her rosy face near as white as Tildy's. "Her pulse and heart are strong, but her breathing is not. I fear for her," she said. "Tildy is in God's hands now."

And mine, thought Matilda. "I will not let you die, Tildy," Matilda said, squeezing her friend's hand. "I know dying means you will go to God, but I do not want you to go. I want you to stay here with me." As Tildy passed from sleep to fretful waking and back again to sleep, Matilda bathed and stroked, warmed and cooled her. Tildy did not know her, but still Matilda talked to her. "Live, Tildy!" she whispered. "There are so many raisin pies we have not eaten, and chicken legs, and fresh bread. And somewhere there is a great lady in a wimple in need of starching looking for a girl just like you."

And Matilda prayed. Her *Aves* and *Pater nosters* could have been piled clear to Heaven, so diligently and ceaselessly did she pray. She called upon Saint Aldegund who defended against fevers, Saint Placid who protected from chills, and Saint Lucy who guarded against loss of blood—and just to be safe, she included Adalbert, Godbert, Swithbert, Matthew, Mark, Luke, and John.

Day after day Matilda sat with Tildy, held her hand, washed her face with cool water, and forced thin porridge between her lips. "I will not let you die, Tildy," Matilda said again and again. "Who will tell me gossip? And try to make me laugh? Do not die. Stay here and make me laugh."

Finally, slowly, Tildy's face passed from pale to pink, and her cheeks from fiery to rose, and her feverish restlessness became quiet sleep.

The next morning Tildy woke, sore but hungry, her fever gone. Matilda leapt up from her doze with a cry that brought the doctor full awake. She examined Tildy's tongue and pulse and the wound on her head. "You should live now," said Margery, "although it appears you will have a mighty scar here on your forehead."

"Gor," said Tildy with a smile, "how tragic I will seem."

Tildy stayed at Margery's while she grew stronger, and Matilda visited often. Once, when Tildy's head tortured her, when she seemed about to go mad with pain, Matilda found herself picking up an apple and peeling it in one long slow spiral while Tildy watched spellbound, her pains and torments for a time forgotten. Matilda reminded herself to thank Tom when next she saw him.

That evening Tildy said to Matilda, "I thank you for your good care of me."

"I would have you live," said Matilda. She did not know how much of Tildy's recovery was due to her good care and how much to her good prayers. But then perhaps it did not matter.

Another day Tildy told Matilda, "Doctor Margery has spoken to Theobald. I will not be returning to his house. She said, 'Can't have Fat Annet heaving any more meat at you.' I will be staying here."

"Does that suit you?"

"Indeed. Doctor Margery is not what I thought a great lady would be. No curls to curl or pleats to stiffen. But great she is, and I can boil and sew and cut linen and sweep for her. It suits me very well, so here I will stay."

Great? Was Doctor Margery great? Well, perhaps she was. "I am pleased for you," Matilda said to Tildy.

Tildy had found a life that suited her. But what about Matilda? If Father Leufredus did not come back, what was she to do? "What am I to do?" she said aloud. "I do not belong here. I am a duck."

"A duck?" Tildy asked.

So Matilda told her of her conversation with Walter. "And Walter said only a duck can lay a duck egg."

"And duck eggs are remarkable indeed," said Tildy with a wink, "for only a duck egg can hatch into a duck."

"So you think a duck is none so bad a thing to be." Tildy smiled. "But I know nothing of what is valued here."

"Nonsense. You know about things I do not even know exist." Tildy yawned and settled herself deeper into Margery's bed. "And you saved my life." She was asleep.

Margery came in as Matilda made ready to leave. She looked at the woman, trying to see again that goose girl who so annoyed her. But she could not. There was Doctor Margery, a physician and a great lady, red of face but kind of eye, sturdy and strong and trustworthy. Matilda said to her, "Tildy does not understand what happened. She thinks it was I saved her life."

"And truly you did."

Matilda shook her head. "I do not have the skills to heal."

"You used the skills you have: your quick thinking, good sense, your strength and your prayers, your friendship. You saved her life, just as surely as if you had mixed the medicine and sewed her wound yourself. You did what you know to do, just as I did what I know."

Matilda thought for a moment. Yes, she had used the tools God gave her, and used them well. "But what you do seems like a miracle," Matilda said finally. "I have no difficulty seeing what ails a struggling fire or a dirty floor, but how can you see what is amiss *inside* of someone?"

The doctor thought a minute and then said, "I see with my hands."

"Your hands?"

"I have no great knowledge of the science of stars or numbers, so I must rely on my eyes, which are limited, and my hands. I can feel your heart pounding in your temples and know when it is too fast. I can feel your skin and know whether you be of cool and moist humor or warm and dry. My hands can tell which lump is but a bruise and which means something is not right, where your stomach is tender or swollen or hot, what bones do not move or fit together as they should—just as Peg's hands can. The hands can see what the eyes cannot."

"Still it sounds like a miracle," said Matilda. Frowning, she looked at her own hands. She could no more see with them than with her feet or her elbows. Well, then, she supposed these were none of her tools. She would work with her own tools, and leave Margery's to Margery. Margery? Would Margery have any patients to use her tools on? "How will you go on without Theobald's help?" Matilda asked her.

"The ills of women are numberless. I have decided there are enough for me to physick without my going to Theobald for patients or advice. The man may know Latin and astrological calculation, but he is a fool when it comes to looking, listening, and tending to people. I will bow to him no longer. I will do what *I* can and do the best I can." Doctor Margery smiled.

"Now let me ask you something. Why was it you fetched me for Tildy? I thought you had no great opinion of me or my skills."

"Because," said Matilda, "I would have Tildy live."

CHAPTER SEVENTEEN

Receiving a Letter

Tom was leaving again. While he was out hitching up Saint Brendan, Matilda remembered him carrying Tildy, and peeling the apple for William Baker, and scrubbing the burned porridge out of the pot for her. She heard Peg snuffle and turned to face her.

"I know *you* do not think much of Tom," Peg said as she wiped her face dry of tears with the hem of her kirtle, "but I do hate to see him go." She snuffled again.

"In truth I believe I have been mistaken about Tom," Matilda said. "He is not a great man of learning, but neither is he witless or villain or wizard. He helps those with no money for physicians or faith in barbers. And I have seen his kindness for myself."

"Better you tell this to Tom," said Peg. "The early-morning air is cool. Here, this cloak is for you, to replace the one you gave away." She wrapped Matilda in russet wool, much like Peg's own best cloak. Matilda nodded her thanks and hurried to the stable. Where had Peg gotten coins for a new cloak?

Tom smiled when he saw her and pulled the raisin bag from his belt. They sat on a straw bale and chewed raisins in silence for a moment or two. She repeated what she had told Peg. "I beg pardon for wronging you," she said.

"Is this your holy priest's opinion?"

"No. It is mine."

"You mean you will not send me to burn at the stake?"

"Not yet," she said smiling, "but you must watch your step."

When Tom and Saint Brendan ambled off, Matilda followed behind, waving and smiling, and then retraced her steps toward Peg's. She had come to realize Blood and Bone Alley was not such a fearful place; neither was it so bad a thing to be helper to a bonesetter. It was not how she wished to spend all her days, but it was not so bad a thing.

As she approached Frog Road, she nearly collided with a tall man dressed in yellow and green. He had squinty blue eyes and a nose that headed south and then changed its mind and turned sharply to the east. He carried a staff and a worn pack on his back. "I seek one Matilda of Blood and Bone Alley," he said. "Can you direct me to her?"

"Indeed," said Matilda. "I am she."

"Then I have for you a letter from Lu . . . Lu . . . Lu something," he said as he handed her a letter.

Father Leufredus. After all this time. She stood perfectly still, except for her heart, which jumped and tumbled in her breast. This letter, she thought, strangely hesitant to open it, would change her life. What might he be saying? *I am most grievously sorry for my delay in answering you, and I beg you to drop everything and hasten to my side, for I have sorely missed you.* She shook her head. He would never say that, even if it were true.

Perhaps, *Come here to me and we will go to Oxford, where your father said there were men of learning and you can consult them about your friend Nathaniel.* But he knew nothing of Nathaniel.

The Pope has named me a saint. Not likely. *The Pope has named you a saint.* Even less likely.

Finally she wiped her hands on her skirt and unfolded the letter.

It was not from Leufredus.

The letter came from a Louis, a Master Louis d'Argent of Oxford. She smiled at the Latin words and began at the beginning:

To the honorable Matilda of the Bone,

I am in receipt of your letter. Do not doubt your value. Your learning is a treasure and a blessing. Cherish it. Homo doctus in se semper divitias habet: *A learned man always has wealth within him.*

As for your Nathaniel Cross, this new world is full of medical marvels and scientific wonders. In Oxford we are experimenting with shiny glass disks which, though hazy and bubbly, help the sight of those who cannot see what is right in front of their faces. Mayhap soon we can help your Nathaniel. Until then he has you.

Vox audita perit, litera scripta manet: *The voice that is heard perishes, the letter that is written remains. Heed me. What you know, what you have learned—use it, value it. It is your wealth.*

Matilda trembled. In Oxford might be help for Nathaniel, but where was help for Matilda? There was no Father Leufredus. He was not coming back for her. Of course. She had known that for a while. But what now?

Dear Saint Thomas, she thought, *who looks after those who have doubts. I am confused and uncertain and I need your help. What is the right thing for me to do now?*

But neither Saint Thomas nor any other saint

answered her, and Matilda knew that, although the saints might provide comfort and consolation, they would not be telling her what life she should live or how she should live it. She must make her own decisions and her own way.

I must think on this. I will get lost, for it ever does help me to think. She walked past the town gate, breathing deeply of the sweet air that smelled of green apples and listening to the birds waking up. Church bells sang. Merchants and farmers entered through the gates, as did peddlers with old fish and young radishes. One old woman slowly pushed a handcart full of parsley and new onions. She stopped to rub her shoulders. "The rheumatics," she explained to Matilda.

"I being attendant on a bonesetter know something of the rheumatics," Matilda told her. "I have heard that it can be cured by carrying with you a stolen potato or four mole feet, although Mistress Peg always recommends poppy tea, warm soaks, and a good hard stretching and bending." The woman nodded her thanks and continued on her way.

Peg. That reminded Matilda, there was much needed doing around Peg's shop. The leather straps on the pulley needed to be oiled before hot weather set in. Marya Cordwainer still owed threepence; she would ignore the debt unless someone brought it to her attention. And

Hag, the cursed cat, should have her leg looked at once more, although it seemed to be healing well.

As Matilda walked and thought, the day grew warm. She took off her new cloak. Now she looked at it, the crooked stitches seemed familiar. And the stain on the hood. *Saliva mucusque!* The cloak was the same color as Peg's because it *was* Peg's, cut down to fit Matilda. Peg would be wearing her old one this winter. Matilda knew that Father Leufredus would never understand or approve of Peg, but in this matter Father Leufredus was wrong. She carefully folded her new cloak, which had been Peg's, given over with love, and she walked quietly for a few moments, face to the sky, the sun on her cheek like the touch of a warm hand.

Turning an unfamiliar corner, she wondered, "Am I lost?" But no. There was water ahead, sparkling in the summer sunshine. She knew this town too well. There was no more getting lost.

The river was a tangle of ships and masts, ferries and barges. Small boats with billowy white sails that snapped in the breeze hurried from here to there and there to here. A family of ducks, quacking furiously, crossed the road, waddled down the riverbank, and launched themselves into the water. Matilda laughed. How extraordinary they were. It was not a bad thing to be a duck. Walter and Tildy had helped her to see that.

And Nathaniel, Tom, and Effie. And Peg. *I must go home and thank Peg for my new cloak,* she thought. *And tell Walter about the ducks, and . . .* It seemed Father Leufredus was right: Becoming attached to people had taken her mind from Heaven. But she was learning to live in God's world.

What would Matilda Bone do now? She did not want to be a bonesetter's helper forever—but she did owe Peg much, and it would be a pleasure to repay her: Peg, dependable as daylight. She wanted to write to this Master Louis and find out more about the magic seeing disks for Nathaniel. Beyond that she did not know, but whatever it was, she believed she could do it. *Can I live not knowing, just believing?* she wondered.

The church bells rang for the hour of Tierce. "Thundering toads!" said Matilda aloud. "I will be late."

Late for what she could not say, but nevertheless she hurried off to meet it, the wind at her back, the same wind that stirred the water, ruffled the feathers of the swimming ducks, and filled the sails of the boats as they hastened up the river to meet what was next.

Author's Note

While researching *Matilda Bone*, I came across much interesting material that I wanted to share, and I included a lot of it in my early drafts. I did realize finally that I was telling a story, not writing a textbook on medieval medicine, so I took out most of it. But here are some of the high points.

We who are accustomed to modern doctors and practices might not even recognize medieval medicine as medicine. Physicians in medieval Europe were not like the doctors we know; they were philosophers, astrologers, numerologists, and dream interpreters. Like most people at that time, they believed in charms, incantations, relics, devils, fairies, gnomes, flying witches, and the power of the unicorn's horn. The earth was thought to be the center of the universe, humans the center of the earth, and fate written in the skies. Physicians studied the positions of the stars and planets, comets and eclipses, and the signs of the zodiac, and made their diagnoses and prognoses accordingly.

In general, none of the medical practitioners understood the benefits of hygiene, nutrition (although many spoke against the evils of gluttony), and public sanitation—or even that there was a connection between these things and health. They did not know about germs, bacteria, or viruses.

Little was known of human anatomy. Dissection of bodies was discouraged by the Church and forbidden by the Koran. There was no means of preserving cadavers, so any dissections that were performed had to be done quickly and in the winter. The few physicians who did open human bodies used what they saw merely to prove what they already believed. X-rays and microscopes did not exist. Knowledge of the circulation of blood was not known until the work of William Harvey in the seventeenth century.

Most people believed that sickness was a result of sin or witchcraft. Souls were considered more important than bodies and were cared for more attentively. There were a few hospitals, but they were shelters for the old and the poor, not centers for medical treatment. Practitioners worked on their own; I found no evidence that indicated the existence of a community such as Blood and Bone Alley, but since shoemakers and potters and weavers gathered together, I imagine that medical people did, too.

Medicine in the Middle Ages was based on Greek, Roman, and Arabic writings and relied heavily on practices that had not changed for two thousand years. Medieval physicians believed in the theory of bodily humors, a theory that had descended unchanged from the ancient Greeks. In the body, it was thought, were four humors—blood, phlegm, yellow bile, and black bile. The humors in balance meant good health. Too much of one or another affected a person's temperament—an excess of blood made a person cheerful; too much phlegm, sluggish; yellow bile, ill-tempered; black bile, melancholy—and led to illness. Treatment consisted mostly of procedures to expel the extra or corrupt humors: bleeding, enemas, diuretics.

Watercasting, or uroscopy (the examination of urine), was of vital importance. Ancient textbooks enumerated the many observations to be made—for example, taste, smell, color, and consistency—for it was believed that every illness or disease in the body was reflected in a person's urine. A physician took a patient's pulse, examined the urine, and made a diagnosis.

Medicines were made and prescribed by physicians and apothecaries. Some medicines were gross (snail shells and eggshells, herbs, and soap for gallstones), some dangerous (broth made from the rags of Egyptian mummies), and others magic (bezoars, stones from the stomach of a goat or cow, believed to counteract poisons). Remedies made from poppies, foxglove, and bread mold most likely were effective; they are the precursors of morphine, digitalis, and penicillin. Other useful practices—using cobwebs to stanch blood, setting and splinting fractures—probably grew from trial and error. Experiments with refraction and magnification led to the development of eyeglasses by the fourteenth century. Considering the reliance on ancient practices, the prohibition of dissections, and medieval practitioners' faith in superstitions, patients were lucky physicians got as much right as they did.

In the Middle Ages the categories of medical practitioners were probably very fluid, nowhere near as rigid as today's medical specialties. Most physicians did no surgery, believing it a profession of low status better left to barbers. Some surgeons were trained; some were closer to butchers than barbers. There were attempts at anesthetics, such as the "soporific sponge," soaked in opium and placed over the patient's nose and mouth, but in general these did not work. Most who had major surgery died. Most wounds festered; most diseases were fatal.

Barber-surgeons cut hair, pulled teeth, treated wounds, and amputated limbs. They advertised their status by wrapping bloody rags about poles in front of their shops. The modern red-and-white-striped barber pole is said to have descended from these early advertisements.

Other medical practitioners included leeches or

bloodletters, who cut veins or used actual leeches to draw off excess blood or corrupt humors, and worm doctors, who believed all illnesses and diseases were caused by worms in the body and sought to destroy those worms without first destroying the patient.

Physical manipulation such as Peg did was often the work of specialists called bonesetters. In England for hundreds of years this work was the special province of great bonesetting families—the Thomases of Liverpool, the Suttons of Norfolk, the Taylors of Lancashire—some still in practice in the nineteenth century. Today such work is done by chiropractors, osteopaths, and orthopedists.

In the Middle Ages most medical practitioners were trained through apprenticeships or experience. Only the most learned, a very small percentage of medieval healers, attended schools. There were medical schools from at least the seventh century in North Africa and the Middle East, most notably at Baghdad and Cairo. The first medical schools in Europe were founded at Cordoba (Spain) by the seventh century and Salerno (Italy) in the tenth century. For a short time in the eleventh century both men and women were trained at Salerno; the most famous Salerno physician was a woman who has come down to us in legend as Trotula, or Dame Trot.

The most educated physicians were not necessarily the best. As Matilda discovered, healing requires more than knowledge and technique. Those like Peg and Tom and Margery who spoke to their patients and listened to the answers, who looked at them carefully, who touched them and developed relationships with them—these were the real healers, regardless of education and reputation.

Although there were relatively few women in the medical professions, they were represented in all fields. Censuses list women physicians, leeches, surgeons, barbers, and apothecaries. Most medical women, however, made up the least prestigious ranks—midwives, wisewomen, herbalists.

In the later Middle Ages merchants and craftsmen began to form themselves into bodies of recognized experts called guilds, which took on a regulatory function. In the fourteenth century so too did physicians. The regulation of medicine led to licensing. This restriction and control meant, on the whole, the regulation of women out of the medical professions. Medical schools did not again accept women until the mid-nineteenth century, and then not without a fight.

As I researched the medieval medical world for *Matilda Bone*, what struck me most about medieval medicine was how fortunate we are not to have to depend on it. Although four hundred years from now physicians might find today's medicine primitive, inefficient, and gross, still I think we are fortunate to have come far enough not to be faced with raven dung on a sore tooth or frog spawn in the eyes.

Books dealing with medieval medicine that I consulted include:

Erwin H. Ackerknecht, M.D. *A Short History of Medicine*. Baltimore: Johns Hopkins University Press, 1982.

Logan Clendening, comp. *Source Book of Medical History*. New York: Dover Publications, 1960.

Nancy Duin and Jenny Sutcliffe. *A History of Medicine: From Pre-History to the Year 2020*. New York: Simon & Schuster, 1992.

Guido Majno, M.D. *The Healing Hand: Man and Wound in the Ancient World*. Cambridge, Mass.: Harvard University Press, 1975.

Steve Parker. *Medicine*. Eyewitness Science series. New York: Dorling Kindersley, 1995.

David Riesman. *The Story of Medicine in the Middle Ages*. New York: Paul B. Hoeber, 1935.

Nancy G. Siraisi. *Medieval and Early Renaissance Medicine: An Introduction to Knowledge and Practice*. Chicago: University of Chicago Press, 1990.